MW01122232

Defoe Abbott Melville Austen
Hugo
Grimm
Christie Chiavelli ontaigne Haggard ooper erson esterton Eliot
Carroll Molière
Stoker
Wilde Maupassant Byron Schiller
Garnett Engels
Goethe Fitzgerald Hawthorne Smith Kafka
Cotton Einstein Dostoyevsky Hall
Baum Kipling Doyle Willis
Leslie Dumas Henry Nietzsche
Flaubert Turgenev Balzac
Stockton Vatsyayana Crane
Burroughs Verne
Curtis Tocqueville Vinci
Homer Widger Tolstoy Gogol Busch
Darwin Whitman
Potter Zola Thoreau Twain Scott Harte
Kant Freud Jowett Stevenson Dickens Plato
Andersen Burton
London Descartes Hesse
Poe Aristotle Wells Cervantes Voltaire Cooke
Hale James Hastings
Bunner Shakespeare
Richter da Chambers Irving
Doré Chekhov Benedict Alcott
Dante Shaw Pushkin
Swift Wodehouse Newton

tredition®

tredition was established in 2006 by Sandra Latusseck and Soenke Schulz. Based in Hamburg, Germany, tredition offers publishing solutions to authors and publishing houses, combined with world-wide distribution of printed and digital book content. tredition is uniquely positioned to enable authors and publishing houses to create books on their own terms and without conventional manu-facturing risks.

For more information please visit: www.tredition.com

TREDITION CLASSICS

This book is part of the TREDITION CLASSICS series. The creators of this series are united by passion for literature and driven by the intention of making all public domain books available in printed format again - worldwide. Most TREDITION CLASSICS titles have been out of print and off the bookstore shelves for decades. At tredi-tion we believe that a great book never goes out of style and that its value is eternal. Several mostly non-profit literature projects pro-vide content to tredition. To support their good work, tredition donates a portion of the proceeds from each sold copy. As a reader of a TREDITION CLASSICS book, you support our mission to save many of the amazing works of world literature from oblivion. See all available books at www.tredition.com.

 Project Gutenberg

The content for this book has been graciously provided by Project Gutenberg. Project Gutenberg is a non-profit organization founded by Michael Hart in 1971 at the University of Illinois. The mission of Project Gutenberg is simple: To encourage the creation and distribu-tion of eBooks. Project Gutenberg is the first and largest collection of public domain eBooks.

All for Love Or, the World Well Lost

A Tragedy

John Dryden

Imprint

This book is part of TREDITION CLASSICS

Author: John Dryden
Cover design: Buchgut, Berlin – Germany

Publisher: tredition GmbH, Hamburg - Germany
ISBN: 978-3-8424-4196-5

www.tredition.com
www.tredition.de

All for Love

by
John Dryden

INTRODUCTORY NOTE

The age of Elizabeth, memorable for so many reasons in the history of England, was especially brilliant in literature, and, within literature, in the drama. With some falling off in spontaneity, the impulse to great dramatic production lasted till the Long Parliament closed the theaters in 1642; and when they were reopened at the Restoration, in 1660, the stage only too faithfully reflected the debased moral tone of the court society of Charles II.

John Dryden (1631-1700), the great representative figure in the literature of the latter part of the seventeenth century, exemplifies in his work most of the main tendencies of the time. He came into notice with a poem on the death of Cromwell in 1658, and two years later was composing couplets expressing his loyalty to the returned king. He married Lady Elizabeth Howard, the daughter of a royalist house, and for practically all the rest of his life remained an adherent of the Tory Party. In 1663 he began writing for the stage, and during the next thirty years he attempted nearly all the current forms of drama. His "Annus Mirabilis" (1666), celebrating the English naval victories over the Dutch, brought him in 1670 the Poet Laureateship. He had, meantime, begun the writing of those admirable critical essays, represented in the present series by his Preface to the "Fables" and his Dedication to the translation of Virgil. In these he shows himself not only a critic of sound and penetrating judgment, but the first master of modern English prose style.

With "Absalom and Achitophel," a satire on the Whig leader, Shaftesbury, Dryden entered a new phase, and achieved what is regarded as "the finest of all political satires." This was followed by "The Medal," again directed against the Whigs, and this by "Mac Flecknoe," a fierce attack on his enemy and rival Shadwell. The Government rewarded his services by a lucrative appointment.

After triumphing in the three fields of drama, criticism, and satire, Dryden appears next as a religious poet in his "Religio Laici," an exposition of the doctrines of the Church of England from a layman's point of view. In the same year that the Catholic James II. ascended the throne, Dryden joined the Roman Church, and two years later defended his new religion in "The Hind and the Panther," an allegorical debate between two animals standing respectively for Catholicism and Anglicanism.

The Revolution of 1688 put an end to Dryden's prosperity; and after a short return to dramatic composition, he turned to translation as a means of supporting himself. He had already done something in this line; and after a series of translations from Juvenal, Persius, and Ovid, he undertook, at the age of sixty-three, the enormous task of turning the entire works of Virgil into English verse. How he succeeded in this, readers of the "Aeneid" in a companion volume of these classics can judge for themselves. Dryden's production closes with the collection of narrative poems called "Fables," published in 1700, in which year he died and was buried in the Poet's Corner in Westminster Abbey.

Dryden lived in an age of reaction against excessive religious idealism, and both his character and his works are marked by the somewhat unheroic traits of such a period. But he was, on the whole, an honest man, open minded, genial, candid, and modest; the wielder of a style, both in verse and prose, unmatched for clearness, vigor, and sanity.

Three types of comedy appeared in England in the time of Dryden — the comedy of humors, the comedy of intrigue, and the comedy of manners — and in all he did work that classed him with the ablest of his contemporaries. He developed the somewhat bombastic type of drama known as the heroic play, and brought it to its height in his "Conquest of Granada"; then, becoming dissatisfied with this form, he cultivated the French classic tragedy on the model of Racine. This he modified by combining with the regularity of the French treatment of dramatic action a richness of characterization in which he showed himself a disciple of Shakespeare, and of this mixed type his best example is "All for Love." Here he has the daring to challenge comparison with his master, and the greatest testimony to his achievement is the fact that, as Professor Noyes has said, "fresh from Shakespeare's 'Antony and Cleopatra,' we can still read with intense pleasure Dryden's version of the story."

DEDICATION

To the Right Honourable, Thomas, Earl of Danby, Viscount Latimer, and Baron Osborne of Kiveton, in Yorkshire; Lord High Treasurer of England, one of His Majesty's Most Honourable Privy Council, and Knight of the Most Noble Order of the Garter.

My Lord,

The gratitude of poets is so troublesome a virtue to great men, that you are often in danger of your own benefits: for you are threatened with some epistle, and not suffered to do good in quiet, or to compound for their silence whom you have obliged. Yet, I confess, I neither am or ought to be surprised at this indulgence; for your lordship has the same right to favour poetry, which the great and noble have ever had —

Carmen amat, quisquis carmine digna gerit.

There is somewhat of a tie in nature betwixt those who are born for worthy actions, and those who can transmit them to posterity; and though ours be much the inferior part, it comes at least within the verge of alliance; nor are we unprofitable members of the commonwealth, when we animate others to those virtues, which we copy and describe from you.

It is indeed their interest, who endeavour the subversion of governments, to discourage poets and historians; for the best which can happen to them, is to be forgotten. But such who, under kings, are the fathers of their country, and by a just and prudent ordering of affairs preserve it, have the same reason to cherish the chroniclers of their actions, as they have to lay up in safety the deeds and evidences of their estates; for such records are their undoubted titles to the love and reverence of after ages. Your lordship's administration has already taken up a considerable part of the English annals; and many of its most happy years are owing to it. His Majesty, the most knowing judge of men, and the best master, has acknowledged the ease and benefit he receives in the incomes of his treasury, which you found not only disordered, but exhausted. All things were in the confusion of a chaos, without form or method, if not reduced beyond it, even to annihilation; so that you had not only to separate the jarring elements, but (if that boldness of expression might be allowed me) to create them. Your enemies had so embroiled the management of your office, that they looked on your advancement as the instrument of your ruin. And as if the clogging of the revenue, and the confusion of accounts, which you found in your entrance, were not sufficient, they added their own weight of malice to the public calamity, by forestalling the credit which should cure it. Your friends on the other side were only capable of pitying, but not of aiding you; no further help or counsel was remaining to you, but what was founded on yourself; and that indeed was your security; for your diligence, your constancy, and your prudence, wrought most surely within, when they were not disturbed by any outward motion. The highest virtue is best to be trusted with itself; for assistance only can be given by a genius superior to that which it assists; and it is the noblest kind of debt, when we are only obliged to God and nature. This then, my lord, is your just commendation, and that you have wrought out yourself a way to glory, by those very means that were designed for your destruction: You have not only restored but advanced the revenues of your master, without grievance to the subject; and, as if that were little yet, the debts of the exchequer, which lay heaviest both on the crown, and on private persons, have by your conduct been established in a certainty of satisfaction. An action so much the more great and honourable, because the case was without the ordinary relief of laws; above the hopes of the afflicted and beyond the narrowness of the treasury to redress, had it been managed by a less able hand. It is certainly the happiest, and most unenvied part of all your fortune, to do good to many, while you do injury to none; to receive at once the prayers of the subject, and the praises of the prince; and, by the care of your conduct, to give him means of exerting the chiefest (if any be the chiefest) of his royal virtues, his distributive justice to the deserving, and his bounty and compassion to the wanting. The disposition of princes towards their people cannot be better discovered than in the choice of their ministers; who, like the animal spirits betwixt the soul and body, participate somewhat of both natures, and make the communication which is betwixt them. A king, who is just and moderate in his nature, who rules according to the laws, whom God has made happy by forming the temper of his soul to the constitution of his government, and who makes us happy, by assuming over us no other sovereignty than that wherein our welfare and liberty consists; a prince, I say, of so excellent a character, and so suitable to the wishes of all good men, could not better have conveyed himself into his people's apprehensions, than in your lordship's person; who so lively express the same virtues, that you seem not so much a copy, as an emanation of him. Moderation is doubtless an establishment of greatness; but there is a steadiness of temper which is likewise requisite in a minister of state; so equal a mixture of both virtues, that he may stand like an isthmus betwixt the two encroaching seas of arbitrary power, and lawless anarchy. The undertaking would be difficult to any but an extraordinary genius, to stand at the line, and to divide the limits; to pay what is due to the great representative of the nation, and neither to enhance, nor to yield up, the undoubted prerogatives of the crown. These, my lord, are the proper virtues of a noble Englishman, as indeed they are properly English virtues; no people in the world being capable of using them, but we who have the happiness to be born under so equal, and so well-poised a government; — a government which has all the advantages of liberty beyond a commonwealth, and all the marks of kingly sovereignty, without the danger of a tyranny. Both my nature, as I am an Englishman, and my reason, as I am a man, have bred in me a loathing to that specious name of a republic; that mock appearance of a liberty, where all who have not part in the government, are slaves; and slaves they are of a viler note, than such as are subjects to an absolute dominion. For no Christian monarchy is so absolute, but it is circumscribed with laws; but when the executive power is in the law-makers, there is no further check upon them; and the people must suffer without a remedy, because they are oppressed by their representatives. If I must serve, the number of my masters, who were born my equals, would but add to the ignominy of my bondage. The nature of our government, above all others, is exactly suited both to the situation of our country, and the temper of the natives; an island being more proper for commerce and for defence, than for extending its dominions on the Continent; for what the valour of its inhabitants might gain, by reason of its remoteness, and the casualties of the seas, it could not so easily preserve: And, therefore, neither the arbitrary power of One, in a monarchy, nor of Many, in a commonwealth, could make us greater than we are. It is true, that vaster and more frequent taxes might be gathered, when the consent of the people was not asked or needed; but this were only by conquering abroad, to be poor at home; and the examples of our neighbours teach us, that they are not always the happiest subjects, whose kings extend their dominions farthest. Since therefore we cannot win by an offensive war, at least, a land war, the model of our government seems naturally contrived for the defensive part; and the consent of a people is easily obtained to contribute to that power which must protect it. Felices nimium, bona si sua norint, Angligenae! And yet there are not wanting malcontents among us, who, surfeiting themselves on too much happiness, would persuade the people that they might be happier by a change. It was indeed the policy of their old forefather, when himself was fallen from the station of glory, to seduce mankind into the same rebellion with him, by telling him he might yet be freer than he was; that is more free than his nature would allow, or, if I may so say, than God could make him. We have already all the liberty which freeborn subjects can enjoy, and all beyond it is but licence. But if it be liberty of conscience which they pretend, the moderation of our church is such, that its practice extends not to the severity of persecution; and its discipline is withal so easy, that it allows more freedom to dissenters than any of the sects would allow to it. In the meantime, what right can be pretended by these men to attempt innovation in church or state? Who made them the trustees, or to speak a little nearer their own language, the keepers of the liberty of England? If their call be extraordinary, let them convince us by working miracles; for ordinary vocation they can have none, to disturb the government under which they were born, and which protects them. He who has often changed his party, and always has made his interest the rule of it, gives little evidence of his sincerity for the public good; it is manifest he changes but for himself, and takes the people for tools to work his fortune. Yet the experience of all ages might let him know, that they who trouble the waters first, have seldom the benefit of the fishing; as they who began the late rebellion enjoyed not the fruit of their undertaking, but were crushed themselves by the usurpation of their own instrument. Neither is it enough for them to answer, that they only intend a reformation of the government, but not the subversion of it: on such pretence all insurrections have been founded; it is striking at the root of power, which is obedience. Every remonstrance of private men has the seed of treason in it; and discourses, which are couched in ambiguous terms, are therefore the more dangerous, because they do all the mischief of open sedition, yet are safe from the punishment of the laws. These, my lord, are considerations, which I should not pass so lightly over, had I room to manage them as they deserve; for no man can be so inconsiderable in a nation, as not to have a share in the welfare of it; and if he be a true Englishman, he must at the same time be fired with indignation, and revenge himself as he can on the disturbers of his country. And to whom could I more fitly apply myself than to your lordship, who have not only an inborn, but an hereditary loyalty? The memorable constancy and sufferings of your father, almost to the ruin of his estate, for the royal cause, were an earnest of that which such a parent and such an institution would produce in the person of a son. But so unhappy an occasion of manifesting your own zeal, in suffering for his present majesty, the providence of God, and the prudence of your administration, will, I hope, prevent; that, as your father's fortune waited on the unhappiness of his sovereign, so your own may participate of the better fate which attends his son. The relation which you have by alliance to the noble family of your lady, serves to confirm to you both this happy augury. For what can deserve a greater place in the English chronicle, than the loyalty and courage, the actions and death, of the general of an army, fighting for his prince and country? The honour and gallantry of the Earl of Lindsey is so illustrious a subject, that it is fit to adorn an heroic poem; for he was the protomartyr of the cause, and the type of his unfortunate royal master.

Yet after all, my lord, if I may speak my thoughts, you are happy rather to us than to yourself; for the multiplicity, the cares, and the vexations of your employment, have betrayed you from yourself, and given you up into the possession of the public. You are robbed of your privacy and friends, and scarce any hour of your life you can call your own. Those, who envy your fortune, if they wanted not good-nature, might more justly pity it; and when they see you watched by a crowd of suitors, whose importunity it is impossible to avoid, would conclude, with reason, that you have lost much more in true content, than you have gained by dignity; and that a private gentleman is better attended by a single servant, than your lordship with so clamorous a train. Pardon me, my lord, if I speak like a philosopher on this subject; the fortune which makes a man uneasy, cannot make him happy; and a wise man must think himself uneasy, when few of his actions are in his choice.

This last consideration has brought me to another, and a very seasonable one for your relief; which is, that while I pity your want of leisure, I have impertinently detained you so long a time. I have put off my own business, which was my dedication, till it is so late, that I am now ashamed to begin it; and therefore I will say nothing of the poem, which I present to you, because I know not if you are like to have an hour, which, with a good conscience, you may throw away in perusing it; and for the author, I have only to beg the continuance of your protection to him, who is,

 My Lord,
  Your Lordship's most obliged,
   Most humble, and
    Most obedient, servant,
     John Dryden.

PREFACE

The death of Antony and Cleopatra is a subject which has been treated by the greatest wits of our nation, after Shakespeare; and by all so variously, that their example has given me the confidence to try myself in this bow of Ulysses amongst the crowd of suitors, and, withal, to take my own measures, in aiming at the mark. I doubt not but the same motive has prevailed with all of us in this attempt; I mean the excellency of the moral: For the chief persons represented were famous patterns of unlawful love; and their end accordingly was unfortunate. All reasonable men have long since concluded, that the hero of the poem ought not to be a character of perfect virtue, for then he could not, without injustice, be made unhappy; nor yet altogether wicked, because he could not then be pitied. I have therefore steered the middle course; and have drawn the character of Antony as favourably as Plutarch, Appian, and Dion Cassius would give me leave; the like I have observed in Cleopatra. That which is wanting to work up the pity to a greater height, was not afforded me by the story; for the crimes of love, which they both committed, were not occasioned by any necessity, or fatal ignorance, but were wholly voluntary; since our passions are, or ought to be, within our power. The fabric of the play is regular enough, as to the inferior parts of it; and the unities of time, place, and action, more exactly observed, than perhaps the English theatre requires. Particularly, the action is so much one, that it is the only one of the kind without episode, or underplot; every scene in the tragedy conducing to the main design, and every act concluding with a turn of it. The greatest error in the contrivance seems to be in the person of Octavia; for, though I might use the privilege of a poet, to introduce her into Alexandria, yet I had not enough considered, that the compassion she moved to herself and children was destructive to that which I reserved for Antony and Cleopatra; whose mutual love being founded upon vice, must lessen the favour of the audience to them, when virtue and innocence were oppressed by it. And, though I justified Antony in some measure, by making Octavia's departure to proceed wholly from herself; yet the force of the first machine still remained; and the dividing of pity, like the cutting of a river into many channels, abated the strength of the natural stream. But this is an objection which none of my critics have urged against me; and therefore I might have let it pass, if I could have resolved to have been partial to myself. The faults my enemies have found are rather cavils concerning little and not essential decencies; which a master of the ceremonies may decide betwixt us. The French poets, I confess, are strict observers of these punctilios: They would not, for example, have suffered Cleopatra and Octavia to have met; or, if they had met, there must have only passed betwixt them some cold civilities, but no eagerness of repartee, for fear of offending against the greatness of their characters, and the modesty of their sex. This objection I foresaw, and at the same time contemned; for I judged it both natural and probable, that Octavia, proud of her new-gained conquest, would search out Cleopatra to triumph over her; and that Cleopatra, thus attacked, was not of a spirit to shun the encounter: And it is not unlikely, that two exasperated rivals should use such satire as I have put into their mouths; for, after all, though the one were a Roman, and the other a queen, they were both women. It is true, some actions, though natural, are not fit to be represented; and broad obscenities in words ought in good manners to be avoided: expressions therefore are a modest clothing of our thoughts, as breeches and petticoats are of our bodies. If I have kept myself within the bounds of modesty, all beyond, it is but nicety and affectation; which is no more but modesty depraved into a vice. They betray themselves who are too quick of apprehension in such cases, and leave all reasonable men to imagine worse of them, than of the poet.

Honest Montaigne goes yet further: Nous ne sommes que ceremonie; la ceremonie nous emporte, et laissons la substance des choses. Nous nous tenons aux branches, et abandonnons le tronc et le corps. Nous avons appris aux dames de rougir, oyans seulement nommer ce qu'elles ne craignent aucunement a faire: Nous n'osons appeller a droit nos membres, et ne craignons pas de les employer a toute sorte de debauche. La ceremonie nous defend d'exprimer par paroles les choses licites et naturelles, et nous l'en croyons; la raison nous defend de n'en faire point d'illicites et mauvaises, et personne ne l'en croit. My comfort is, that by this opinion my enemies are but sucking critics, who would fain be nibbling ere their teeth are come.

Yet, in this nicety of manners does the excellency of French poetry consist. Their heroes are the most civil people breathing; but their good breeding seldom extends to a word of sense; all their wit is in their ceremony; they want the genius which animates our stage; and therefore it is but necessary, when they cannot please, that they should take care not to offend. But as the civilest man in the company is commonly the dullest, so these authors, while they are afraid to make you laugh or cry, out of pure good manners make you sleep. They are so careful not to exasperate a critic, that they never leave him any work; so busy with the broom, and make so clean a riddance that there is little left either for censure or for praise: For no part of a poem is worth our discommending, where the whole is insipid; as when we have once tasted of palled wine, we stay not to examine it glass by glass. But while they affect to shine in trifles, they are often careless in essentials. Thus, their Hippolytus is so scrupulous in point of decency, that he will rather expose himself to death, than accuse his stepmother to his father; and my critics I am sure will commend him for it. But we of grosser apprehensions are apt to think that this excess of generosity is not practicable, but with fools and madmen. This was good manners with a vengeance; and the audience is like to be much concerned at the misfortunes of this admirable hero. But take Hippolytus out of his poetic fit, and I suppose he would think it a wiser part to set the saddle on the right horse, and choose rather to live with the reputation of a plain-spoken, honest man, than to die with the infamy of an incestuous villain. In the meantime we may take notice, that where the poet ought to have preserved the character as it was delivered to us by antiquity, when he should have given us the picture of a rough young man, of the Amazonian strain, a jolly huntsman, and both by his profession and his early rising a mortal enemy to love, he has chosen to give him the turn of gallantry, sent him to travel from Athens to Paris, taught him to make love, and transformed the Hippolytus of Euripides into Monsieur Hippolyte. I should not have troubled myself thus far with French poets, but that I find our Chedreux critics wholly form their judgments by them. But for my part, I desire to be tried by the laws of my own country; for it seems unjust to me, that the French should prescribe here, till they have conquered. Our little sonneteers, who follow them, have too narrow souls to judge of poetry. Poets themselves are the most proper, though I conclude not the only critics. But till some genius, as universal as Aristotle, shall arise, one who can penetrate into all arts and sciences, without the practice of them, I shall think it reasonable, that the judgment of an artificer in his own art should be preferable to the opinion of another man; at least where he is not bribed by interest, or prejudiced by malice. And this, I suppose, is manifest by plain inductions: For, first, the crowd cannot be presumed to have more than a gross instinct of what pleases or displeases them: Every man will grant me this; but then, by a particular kindness to himself, he draws his own stake first, and will be distinguished from the multitude, of which other men may think him one. But, if I come closer to those who are allowed for witty men, either by the advantage of their quality, or by common fame, and affirm that neither are they qualified to decide sovereignly concerning poetry, I shall yet have a strong party of my opinion; for most of them severally will exclude the rest, either from the number of witty men, or at least of able judges. But here again they are all indulgent to themselves; and every one who believes himself a wit, that is, every man, will pretend at the same time to a right of judging. But to press it yet further, there are many witty men, but few poets; neither have all poets a taste of tragedy. And this is the rock on which they are daily splitting. Poetry, which is a picture of nature, must generally please; but it is not to be understood that all parts of it must please every man; therefore is not tragedy to be judged by a witty man, whose taste is only confined to comedy. Nor is every man, who loves tragedy, a sufficient judge of it; he must understand the excellences of it too, or he will only prove a blind admirer, not a critic. From hence it comes that so many satires on poets, and censures of their writings, fly abroad. Men of pleasant conversation (at least esteemed so), and endued with a trifling kind of fancy, perhaps helped out with some smattering of Latin, are ambitious to distinguish themselves from the herd of gentlemen, by their poetry —

Rarus enim ferme sensus communis in illa Fortuna.

And is not this a wretched affectation, not to be contented with what fortune has done for them, and sit down quietly with their estates, but they must call their wits in question, and needlessly expose their nakedness to public view? Not considering that they are not to expect the same approbation from sober men, which they have found from their flatterers after the third bottle. If a little glittering in discourse has passed them on us for witty men, where was the necessity of undeceiving the world? Would a man who has an ill title to an estate, but yet is in possession of it; would he bring it of his own accord, to be tried at Westminster? We who write, if we want the talent, yet have the excuse that we do it for a poor subsistence; but what can be urged in their defence, who, not having the vocation of poverty to scribble, out of mere wantonness take pains to make themselves ridiculous? Horace was certainly in the right, where he said, "That no man is satisfied with his own condition." A poet is not pleased, because he is not rich; and the rich are discontented, because the poets will not admit them of their number. Thus the case is hard with writers: If they succeed not, they must starve; and if they do, some malicious satire is prepared to level them, for daring to please without their leave. But while they are so eager to destroy the fame of others, their ambition is manifest in their concernment; some poem of their own is to be produced, and the slaves are to be laid flat with their faces on the ground, that the monarch may appear in the greater majesty.

Dionysius and Nero had the same longings, but with all their power they could never bring their business well about. 'Tis true, they proclaimed themselves poets by sound of trumpet; and poets they were, upon pain of death to any man who durst call them otherwise. The audience had a fine time on't, you may imagine; they sat in a bodily fear, and looked as demurely as they could: for it was a hanging matter to laugh unseasonably; and the tyrants were suspicious, as they had reason, that their subjects had them in the wind; so, every man, in his own defence, set as good a face upon the business as he could. It was known beforehand that the monarchs were to be crowned laureates; but when the show was over, and an honest man was suffered to depart quietly, he took out his laughter which he had stifled, with a firm resolution never more to see an emperor's play, though he had been ten years a-making it. In the meantime the true poets were they who made the best markets: for they had wit enough to yield the prize with a good grace, and not contend with him who had thirty legions. They were sure to be rewarded, if they confessed themselves bad writers, and that was somewhat better than to be martyrs for their reputation. Lucan's example was enough to teach them manners; and after he was put to death, for overcoming Nero, the emperor carried it without dispute for the best poet in his dominions. No man was ambitious of that grinning honour; for if he heard the malicious trumpeter proclaiming his name before his betters, he knew there was but one way with him. Maecenas took another course, and we know he was more than a great man, for he was witty too: But finding himself far gone in poetry, which Seneca assures us was not his talent, he thought it his best way to be well with Virgil and with Horace; that at least he might be a poet at the second hand; and we see how happily it has succeeded with him; for his own bad poetry is forgotten, and their panegyrics of him still remain. But they who should be our patrons are for no such expensive ways to fame; they have much of the poetry of Maecenas, but little of his liberality. They are for prosecuting Horace and Virgil, in the persons of their successors; for such is every man who has any part of their soul and fire, though in a less degree. Some of their little zanies yet go further; for they are persecutors even of Horace himself, as far as they are able, by their ignorant and vile imitations of him; by making an unjust use of his authority, and turning his artillery against his friends. But how would he disdain to be copied by such hands! I dare answer for him, he would be more uneasy in their company, than he was with Crispinus, their forefather, in the Holy Way; and would no more have allowed them a place amongst the critics, than he would Demetrius the mimic, and Tigellius the buffoon;

— — —- Demetri, teque, Tigelli,
Discipulorum inter jubeo plorare cathedras.

With what scorn would he look down on such miserable translators, who make doggerel of his Latin, mistake his meaning, misapply his censures, and often contradict their own? He is fixed as a landmark to set out the bounds of poetry —

— — —- Saxum antiquum, ingens, —
Limes agro positus, litem ut discerneret arvis.

But other arms than theirs, and other sinews are required, to raise the weight of such an author; and when they would toss him against enemies—

Genua labant, gelidus concrevit frigore sanguis.
Tum lapis ipse viri, vacuum per inane volatus,
Nec spatium evasit totum, nec pertulit ictum.

For my part, I would wish no other revenge, either for myself, or the rest of the poets, from this rhyming judge of the twelve-penny gallery, this legitimate son of Sternhold, than that he would subscribe his name to his censure, or (not to tax him beyond his learning) set his mark: For, should he own himself publicly, and come from behind the lion's skin, they whom he condemns would be thankful to him, they whom he praises would choose to be condemned; and the magistrates, whom he has elected, would modestly withdraw from their employment, to avoid the scandal of his nomination. The sharpness of his satire, next to himself, falls most heavily on his friends, and they ought never to forgive him for commending them perpetually the wrong way, and sometimes by contraries. If he have a friend, whose hastiness in writing is his greatest fault, Horace would have taught him to have minced the matter, and to have called it readiness of thought, and a flowing fancy; for friendship will allow a man to christen an imperfection by the name of some neighbour virtue—

Vellem in amicitia sic erraremus; et isti
Errori nomen virtus posuisset honestum.

But he would never allowed him to have called a slow man hasty, or a hasty writer a slow drudge, as Juvenal explains it—

— — —- Canibus pigris, scabieque vestusta
Laevibus, et siccae lambentibus ora lucernae,
Nomen erit, Pardus, Tigris, Leo; si quid adhuc est
Quod fremit in terris violentius.

Yet Lucretius laughs at a foolish lover, even for excusing the imperfections of his mistress—

Nigra <melichroos> est, immunda et foetida <akosmos>
Balba loqui non quit, <traylizei>; muta pudens est, etc.

But to drive it ad Aethiopem cygnum is not to be endured. I leave him to interpret this by the benefit of his French version on the other side, and without further considering him, than I have the rest of my illiterate censors, whom I have disdained to answer, because they are not qualified for judges. It remains that I acquaint the reader, that I have endeavoured in this play to follow the practice of the ancients, who, as Mr. Rymer has judiciously observed, are and ought to be our masters. Horace likewise gives it for a rule in his art of poetry —

— — —- Vos exemplaria Graeca
Nocturna versate manu, versate diurna.

Yet, though their models are regular, they are too little for English tragedy; which requires to be built in a larger compass. I could give an instance in the Oedipus Tyrannus, which was the masterpiece of Sophocles; but I reserve it for a more fit occasion, which I hope to have hereafter. In my style, I have professed to imitate the divine Shakespeare; which that I might perform more freely, I have disencumbered myself from rhyme. Not that I condemn my former way, but that this is more proper to my present purpose. I hope I need not to explain myself, that I have not copied my author servilely: Words and phrases must of necessity receive a change in succeeding ages; but it is almost a miracle that much of his language remains so pure; and that he who began dramatic poetry amongst us, untaught by any, and as Ben Jonson tells us, without learning, should by the force of his own genius perform so much, that in a manner he has left no praise for any who come after him. The occasion is fair, and the subject would be pleasant to handle the difference of styles betwixt him and Fletcher, and wherein, and how far they are both to be imitated. But since I must not be over-confident of my own performance after him, it will be prudence in me to be silent. Yet, I hope, I may affirm, and without vanity, that, by imitating him, I have excelled myself throughout the play; and particularly, that I prefer the scene betwixt Antony and Ventidius in the first act, to anything which I have written in this kind.

PROLOGUE

What flocks of critics hover here to-day,
As vultures wait on armies for their prey,
All gaping for the carcase of a play!
With croaking notes they bode some dire event,
And follow dying poets by the scent.
Ours gives himself for gone; y' have watched your time:
He fights this day unarmed, — without his rhyme; —
And brings a tale which often has been told;
As sad as Dido's; and almost as old.
His hero, whom you wits his bully call,
Bates of his mettle, and scarce rants at all;
He's somewhat lewd; but a well-meaning mind;
Weeps much; fights little; but is wond'rous kind.
In short, a pattern, and companion fit,
For all the keeping Tonies of the pit.
I could name more: a wife, and mistress too;
Both (to be plain) too good for most of you:
The wife well-natured, and the mistress true.
  Now, poets, if your fame has been his care,
Allow him all the candour you can spare.
A brave man scorns to quarrel once a day;
Like Hectors in at every petty fray.
Let those find fault whose wit's so very small,
They've need to show that they can think at all;
Errors, like straws, upon the surface flow;
He who would search for pearls, must dive below.
Fops may have leave to level all they can;
As pigmies would be glad to lop a man.
Half-wits are fleas; so little and so light,
We scarce could know they live, but that they bite.
But, as the rich, when tired with daily feasts,
For change, become their next poor tenant's guests;
Drink hearty draughts of ale from plain brown bowls,
And snatch the homely rasher from the coals:
So you, retiring from much better cheer,

For once, may venture to do penance here.
And since that plenteous autumn now is past,
Whose grapes and peaches have indulged your taste,
Take in good part, from our poor poet's board,
Such rivelled fruits as winter can afford.

.

ALL FOR LOVE

or

THE WORLD WELL LOST

A TRAGEDY

DRAMATIS PERSONAE

MARK ANTONY.
VENTIDIUS, his General.
DOLABELLA, his Friend.
ALEXAS, the Queen's Eunuch.
SERAPION, Priest of Isis.
MYRIS, another Priest.
Servants to Antony.

CLEOPATRA, Queen of Egypt.
OCTAVIA, Antony's Wife.
CHARMION, Cleopatra's Maid.
IRAS, Cleopatra's Maid.
Antony's two little Daughters.

SCENE. — Alexandria.

Act I

Scene I. — The Temple of Isis

Enter SERAPION, MYRIS, Priests of Isis

SERAPION. Portents and prodigies have grown so frequent,
That they have lost their name. Our fruitful Nile
Flowed ere the wonted season, with a torrent
So unexpected, and so wondrous fierce,
That the wild deluge overtook the haste
Even of the hinds that watched it: Men and beasts
Were borne above the tops of trees, that grew
On the utmost margin of the water-mark.
Then, with so swift an ebb the flood drove backward,
It slipt from underneath the scaly herd:
Here monstrous phocae panted on the shore;
Forsaken dolphins there with their broad tails,
Lay lashing the departing waves: hard by them,
Sea horses floundering in the slimy mud,
Tossed up their heads, and dashed the ooze about them.

Enter ALEXAS behind them

MYRIS. Avert these omens, Heaven!

SERAPION. Last night, between the hours of twelve and one,
In a lone aisle of the temple while I walked,
A whirlwind rose, that, with a violent blast,
Shook all the dome: the doors around me clapt;
The iron wicket, that defends the vault,
Where the long race of Ptolemies is laid,
Burst open, and disclosed the mighty dead.
From out each monument, in order placed,
An armed ghost starts up: the boy-king last
Reared his inglorious head. A peal of groans

Then followed, and a lamentable voice
Cried, Egypt is no more! My blood ran back,
My shaking knees against each other knocked;
On the cold pavement down I fell entranced,
And so unfinished left the horrid scene.

ALEXAS. And dreamed you this? or did invent the story,
    [Showing himself.]
To frighten our Egyptian boys withal,
And train them up, betimes, in fear of priesthood?

SERAPION. My lord, I saw you not,
Nor meant my words should reach you ears; but what
I uttered was most true.

ALEXAS. A foolish dream,
Bred from the fumes of indigested feasts,
And holy luxury.

SERAPION. I know my duty:
This goes no further.

ALEXAS. 'Tis not fit it should;
Nor would the times now bear it, were it true.
All southern, from yon hills, the Roman camp
Hangs o'er us black and threatening like a storm
Just breaking on our heads.

SERAPION. Our faint Egyptians pray for Antony;
But in their servile hearts they own Octavius.

MYRIS. Why then does Antony dream out his hours,
And tempts not fortune for a noble day,
Which might redeem what Actium lost?

ALEXAS. He thinks 'tis past recovery.

SERAPION. Yet the foe
Seems not to press the siege.

ALEXAS. Oh, there's the wonder.
Maecenas and Agrippa, who can most
With Caesar, are his foes. His wife Octavia,
Driven from his house, solicits her revenge;
And Dolabella, who was once his friend,
Upon some private grudge, now seeks his ruin:
Yet still war seems on either side to sleep.

SERAPION. 'Tis strange that Antony, for some days past,
Has not beheld the face of Cleopatra;
But here, in Isis' temple, lives retired,
And makes his heart a prey to black despair.

ALEXAS. 'Tis true; and we much fear he hopes by absence
To cure his mind of love.

SERAPION. If he be vanquished,
Or make his peace, Egypt is doomed to be
A Roman province; and our plenteous harvests
Must then redeem the scarceness of their soil.
While Antony stood firm, our Alexandria
Rivalled proud Rome (dominion's other seat),
And fortune striding, like a vast Colossus,
Could fix an equal foot of empire here.

ALEXAS. Had I my wish, these tyrants of all nature,
Who lord it o'er mankind, rhould perish, — perish,
Each by the other's sword; But, since our will
Is lamely followed by our power, we must
Depend on one; with him to rise or fall.

SERAPION. How stands the queen affected?

ALEXAS. Oh, she dotes,
She dotes, Serapion, on this vanquished man,
And winds herself about his mighty ruins;
Whom would she yet forsake, yet yield him up,
This hunted prey, to his pursuer's hands,
She might preserve us all: but 'tis in vain—
This changes my designs, this blasts my counsels,
And makes me use all means to keep him here.
Whom I could wish divided from her arms,
Far as the earth's deep centre. Well, you know
The state of things; no more of your ill omens
And black prognostics; labour to confirm
The people's hearts.

Enter VENTIDIUS, talking aside with a Gentleman of ANTONY'S

SERAPION. These Romans will o'erhear us.
But who's that stranger? By his warlike port,
His fierce demeanour, and erected look,
He's of no vulgar note.

ALEXAS. Oh, 'tis Ventidius,
Our emperor's great lieutenant in the East,
Who first showed Rome that Parthia could be conquered.
When Antony returned from Syria last,
He left this man to guard the Roman frontiers.

SERAPION. You seem to know him well.

ALEXAS. Too well. I saw him at Cilicia first,
When Cleopatra there met Antony:
A mortal foe was to us, and Egypt.
But,—let me witness to the worth I hate,—
A braver Roman never drew a sword;
Firm to his prince, but as a friend, not slave,
He ne'er was of his pleasures; but presides
O'er all his cooler hours, and morning counsels:

In short the plainness, fierceness, rugged virtue,
Of an old true-stampt Roman lives in him.
His coming bodes I know not what of ill
To our affairs. Withdraw to mark him better;
And I'll acquaint you why I sought you here,
And what's our present work.

    [They withdraw to a corner of the stage; and VENTIDIUS,
      with the other, comes forward to the front.]

VENTIDIUS. Not see him; say you?
I say, I must, and will.

GENTLEMAN. He has commanded,
On pain of death, none should approach his presence.

VENTIDIUS. I bring him news will raise his drooping spirits,
Give him new life.

 GENTLEMAN. He sees not Cleopatra.

 VENTIDIUS. Would he had never seen her!

GENTLEMAN. He eats not, drinks not, sleeps not, has no use
Of anything, but thought; or if he talks,
'Tis to himself, and then 'tis perfect raving:
Then he defies the world, and bids it pass,
Sometimes he gnaws his lips, and curses loud
The boy Octavius; then he draws his mouth
Into a scornful smile, and cries, "Take all,
The world's not worth my care."

VENTIDIUS. Just, just his nature.
Virtue's his path; but sometimes 'tis too narrow
For his vast soul; and then he starts out wide,
And bounds into a vice, that bears him far
From his first course, and plunges him in ills:
But, when his danger makes him find his faults,

Quick to observe, and full of sharp remorse,
He censures eagerly his own misdeeds,
Judging himself with malice to himself,
And not forgiving what as man he did,
Because his other parts are more than man. —
He must not thus be lost.

[ALEXAS and the Priests come forward.]

ALEXAS. You have your full instructions, now advance,
Proclaim your orders loudly.

SERAPION. Romans, Egyptians, hear the queen's command.
Thus Cleopatra bids: Let labour cease;
To pomp and triumphs give this happy day,
That gave the world a lord: 'tis Antony's.
Live, Antony; and Cleopatra live!
Be this the general voice sent up to heaven,
And every public place repeat this echo.

VENTIDIUS. Fine pageantry!
[Aside.]

SERAPION. Set out before your doors
The images of all your sleeping fathers,
With laurels crowned; with laurels wreath your posts,
And strew with flowers the pavement; let the priests
Do present sacrifice; pour out the wine,
And call the gods to join with you in gladness.

VENTIDIUS. Curse on the tongue that bids this general joy!
Can they be friends of Antony, who revel
When Antony's in danger? Hide, for shame,
You Romans, your great grandsires' images,
For fear their souls should animate their marbles,
To blush at their degenerate progeny.

ALEXAS. A love, which knows no bounds, to Antony,
Would mark the day with honours, when all heaven
Laboured for him, when each propitious star
Stood wakeful in his orb, to watch that hour
And shed his better influence. Her own birthday
Our queen neglected like a vulgar fate,
That passed obscurely by.

VENTIDIUS. Would it had slept,
Divided far from his; till some remote
And future age had called it out, to ruin
Some other prince, not him!

ALEXAS. Your emperor,
Though grown unkind, would be more gentle, than
To upbraid my queen for loving him too well.

VENTIDIUS. Does the mute sacrifice upbraid the priest!
He knows him not his executioner.
Oh, she has decked his ruin with her love,
Led him in golden bands to gaudy slaughter,
And made perdition pleasing: She has left him
The blank of what he was.
I tell thee, eunuch, she has quite unmanned him.
Can any Roman see, and know him now,
Thus altered from the lord of half mankind,
Unbent, unsinewed, made a woman's toy,
Shrunk from the vast extent of all his honours,
And crampt within a corner of the world?
O Antony!
Thou bravest soldier, and thou best of friends!
Bounteous as nature; next to nature's God!
Couldst thou but make new worlds, so wouldst thou give them,
As bounty were thy being! rough in battle,
As the first Romans when they went to war;
Yet after victory more pitiful

Than all their praying virgins left at home!

ALEXAS. Would you could add, to those more shining virtues,
His truth to her who loves him.

VENTIDIUS. Would I could not!
But wherefore waste I precious hours with thee!
Thou art her darling mischief, her chief engine,
Antony's other fate. Go, tell thy queen,
Ventidius is arrived, to end her charms.
Let your Egyptian timbrels play alone,
Nor mix effeminate sounds with Roman trumpets,
You dare not fight for Antony; go pray
And keep your cowards' holiday in temples.
    [Exeunt ALEXAS, SERAPION.]

 Re-enter the Gentleman of M. ANTONY

2 Gent. The emperor approaches, and commands,
On pain of death, that none presume to stay.

1 Gent. I dare not disobey him.
    [Going out with the other.]

VENTIDIUS. Well, I dare.
But I'll observe him first unseen, and find
Which way his humour drives: The rest I'll venture.
    [Withdraws.]

    Enter ANTONY, walking with a disturbed motion before
    he speaks

ANTONY. They tell me, 'tis my birthday, and I'll keep it
With double pomp of sadness.
'Tis what the day deserves, which gave me breath.
Why was I raised the meteor of the world,

Hung in the skies, and blazing as I travelled,
'Till all my fires were spent; and then cast downward,
To be trod out by Caesar?

VENTIDIUS. [aside.] On my soul,
'Tis mournful, wondrous mournful!

ANTONY. Count thy gains.
Now, Antony, wouldst thou be born for this?
Glutton of fortune, thy devouring youth
Has starved thy wanting age.

VENTIDIUS. How sorrow shakes him!
    [Aside.]
So, now the tempest tears him up by the roots,
And on the ground extends the noble ruin.
    [ANTONY having thrown himself down.]
Lie there, thou shadow of an emperor;
The place thou pressest on thy mother earth
Is all thy empire now: now it contains thee;
Some few days hence, and then 'twill be too large,
When thou'rt contracted in thy narrow urn,
Shrunk to a few ashes; then Octavia
(For Cleopatra will not live to see it),
Octavia then will have thee all her own,
And bear thee in her widowed hand to Caesar;
Caesar will weep, the crocodile will weep,
To see his rival of the universe
Lie still and peaceful there. I'll think no more on't.

ANTONY. Give me some music, look that it be sad.
I'll soothe my melancholy, till I swell,
And burst myself with sighing. —
    [Soft music.]
'Tis somewhat to my humour; stay, I fancy
I'm now turned wild, a commoner of nature;
Of all forsaken, and forsaking all;

Live in a shady forest's sylvan scene,
Stretched at my length beneath some blasted oak,
I lean my head upon the mossy bark,
And look just of a piece as I grew from it;
My uncombed locks, matted like mistletoe,
Hang o'er my hoary face; a murm'ring brook
Runs at my foot.

VENTIDIUS. Methinks I fancy
Myself there too.

ANTONY. The herd come jumping by me,
And fearless, quench their thirst, while I look on,
And take me for their fellow-citizen.
More of this image, more; it lulls my thoughts.
    [Soft music again.]

VENTIDIUS. I must disturb him; I can hold no longer.
    [Stands before him.]

ANTONY. [starting up]. Art thou Ventidius?

VENTIDIUS. Are you Antony?
I'm liker what I was, than you to him
I left you last.

ANTONY. I'm angry.

VENTIDIUS. So am I.

ANTONY. I would be private: leave me.

VENTIDIUS. Sir, I love you,
And therefore will not leave you.

ANTONY. Will not leave me!
Where have you learnt that answer? Who am I?

VENTIDIUS. My emperor; the man I love next Heaven:
If I said more, I think 'twere scare a sin:
You're all that's good, and god-like.

ANTONY. All that's wretched.
You will not leave me then?

VENTIDIUS. 'Twas too presuming
To say I would not; but I dare not leave you:
And, 'tis unkind in you to chide me hence
So soon, when I so far have come to see you.

ANTONY. Now thou hast seen me, art thou satisfied?
For, if a friend, thou hast beheld enough;
And, if a foe, too much.

VENTIDIUS. Look, emperor, this is no common dew.
    [Weeping.]
I have not wept this forty years; but now
My mother comes afresh into my eyes;
I cannot help her softness.

ANTONY. By heavens, he weeps! poor good old man, he weeps!
The big round drops course one another down
The furrows of his cheeks. — Stop them, Ventidius,
Or I shall blush to death, they set my shame,
That caused them, full before me.

 VENTIDIUS. I'll do my best.

ANTONY. Sure there's contagion in the tears of friends:
See, I have caught it too. Believe me, 'tis not
For my own griefs, but thine. — Nay, father!

 VENTIDIUS. Emperor.

ANTONY. Emperor! Why, that's the style of victory;
The conqu'ring soldier, red with unfelt wounds,
Salutes his general so; but never more
Shall that sound reach my ears.

VENTIDIUS. I warrant you.

ANTONY. Actium, Actium! Oh! —

VENTIDIUS. It sits too near you.

ANTONY. Here, here it lies a lump of lead by day,
And, in my short, distracted, nightly slumbers,
The hag that rides my dreams. —

VENTIDIUS. Out with it; give it vent.

ANTONY. Urge not my shame.
I lost a battle, —

VENTIDIUS. So has Julius done.

ANTONY. Thou favour'st me, and speak'st not half thou think'st;
For Julius fought it out, and lost it fairly.
But Antony —

VENTIDIUS. Nay, stop not.

ANTONY. Antony —
Well, thou wilt have it, — like a coward, fled,
Fled while his soldiers fought; fled first, Ventidius.
Thou long'st to curse me, and I give thee leave.
I know thou cam'st prepared to rail.

VENTIDIUS. I did.

ANTONY. I'll help thee. — I have been a man, Ventidius.

VENTIDIUS. Yes, and a brave one! but —

ANTONY. I know thy meaning.
But I have lost my reason, have disgraced
The name of soldier, with inglorious ease.
In the full vintage of my flowing honours,
Sat still, and saw it prest by other hands.
Fortune came smiling to my youth, and wooed it,
And purple greatness met my ripened years.
When first I came to empire, I was borne
On tides of people, crowding to my triumphs;
The wish of nations, and the willing world
Received me as its pledge of future peace;
I was so great, so happy, so beloved,
Fate could not ruin me; till I took pains,
And worked against my fortune, child her from me,
And returned her loose; yet still she came again.
My careless days, and my luxurious nights,
At length have wearied her, and now she's gone,
Gone, gone, divorced for ever. Help me, soldier,
To curse this madman, this industrious fool,
Who laboured to be wretched: Pr'ythee, curse me.

VENTIDIUS. No.

ANTONY. Why?

VENTIDIUS. You are too sensible already
Of what you've done, too conscious of your failings;
And, like a scorpion, whipt by others first
To fury, sting yourself in mad revenge.
I would bring balm, and pour it in your wounds,
Cure your distempered mind, and heal your fortunes.

ANTONY. I know thou would'st.

VENTIDIUS. I will.

ANTONY. Ha, ha, ha, ha!

VENTIDIUS. You laugh.

ANTONY. I do, to see officious love.
Give cordials to the dead.

VENTIDIUS. You would be lost, then?

ANTONY. I am.

VENTIDIUS. I say you are not. Try your fortune.

ANTONY. I have, to the utmost. Dost thou think me desperate,
Without just cause? No, when I found all lost
Beyond repair, I hid me from the world,
And learnt to scorn it here; which now I do
So heartily, I think it is not worth
The cost of keeping.

VENTIDIUS. Caesar thinks not so;
He'll thank you for the gift he could not take.
You would be killed like Tully, would you? do,
Hold out your throat to Caesar, and die tamely.

ANTONY. No, I can kill myself; and so resolve.

VENTIDIUS. I can die with you too, when time shall serve;
But fortune calls upon us now to live,
To fight, to conquer.

ANTONY. Sure thou dream'st, Ventidius.

VENTIDIUS. No; 'tis you dream; you sleep away your hours
In desperate sloth, miscalled philosophy.
Up, up, for honour's sake; twelve legions wait you,
And long to call you chief: By painful journeys
I led them, patient both of heat and hunger,
Down form the Parthian marches to the Nile.
'Twill do you good to see their sunburnt faces,
Their scarred cheeks, and chopt hands: there's virtue in them.
They'll sell those mangled limbs at dearer rates
Than yon trim bands can buy.

ANTONY. Where left you them?

VENTIDIUS. I said in Lower Syria.

ANTONY. Bring them hither;
There may be life in these.

VENTIDIUS. They will not come.

ANTONY. Why didst thou mock my hopes with promised aids,
To double my despair? They're mutinous.

VENTIDIUS. Most firm and loyal.

ANTONY. Yet they will not march
To succour me. O trifler!

VENTIDIUS. They petition
You would make haste to head them.

ANTONY. I'm besieged.

VENTIDIUS. There's but one way shut up: How came I hither?

ANTONY. I will not stir.

VENTIDIUS. They would perhaps desire
A better reason.

ANTONY. I have never used
My soldiers to demand a reason of
My actions. Why did they refuse to march?

VENTIDIUS. They said they would not fight for Cleopatra.

ANTONY. What was't they said?

VENTIDIUS. They said they would not fight for Cleopatra.
Why should they fight indeed, to make her conquer,
And make you more a slave? to gain you kingdoms,
Which, for a kiss, at your next midnight feast,

You'll sell to her? Then she new-names her jewels,
And calls this diamond such or such a tax;
Each pendant in her ear shall be a province.

ANTONY. Ventidius, I allow your tongue free licence
On all my other faults; but, on your life,
No word of Cleopatra: she deserves
More worlds than I can lose.

VENTIDIUS. Behold, you Powers,
To whom you have intrusted humankind!
See Europe, Afric, Asia, put in balance,
And all weighed down by one light, worthless woman!
I think the gods are Antonies, and give,
Like prodigals, this nether world away
To none but wasteful hands.

ANTONY. You grow presumptuous.

VENTIDIUS. I take the privilege of plain love to speak.

ANTONY. Plain love! plain arrogance, plain insolence!
Thy men are cowards; thou, an envious traitor;
Who, under seeming honesty, hast vented
The burden of thy rank, o'erflowing gall.
O that thou wert my equal; great in arms
As the first Caesar was, that I might kill thee
Without a stain to honour!

VENTIDIUS. You may kill me;
You have done more already, — called me traitor.

ANTONY. Art thou not one?

VENTIDIUS. For showing you yourself,
Which none else durst have done? but had I been
That name, which I disdain to speak again,
I needed not have sought your abject fortunes,

Come to partake your fate, to die with you.
What hindered me to have led my conquering eagles
To fill Octavius' bands? I could have been
A traitor then, a glorious, happy traitor,
And not have been so called.

ANTONY. Forgive me, soldier;
I've been too passionate.

VENTIDIUS. You thought me false;
Thought my old age betrayed you: Kill me, sir,
Pray, kill me; yet you need not, your unkindness
Has left your sword no work.

ANTONY. I did not think so;
I said it in my rage: Pr'ythee, forgive me.
Why didst thou tempt my anger, by discovery
Of what I would not hear?

VENTIDIUS. No prince but you
Could merit that sincerity I used,
Nor durst another man have ventured it;
But you, ere love misled your wandering eyes,
Were sure the chief and best of human race,
Framed in the very pride and boast of nature;
So perfect, that the gods, who formed you, wondered
At their own skill, and cried—A lucky hit
Has mended our design. Their envy hindered,
Else you had been immortal, and a pattern,
When Heaven would work for ostentation's sake
To copy out again.

ANTONY. But Cleopatra—
Go on; for I can bear it now.

VENTIDIUS. No more.

ANTONY. Thou dar'st not trust my passion, but thou may'st;
Thou only lov'st, the rest have flattered me.

VENTIDIUS. Heaven's blessing on your heart for that kind word!
May I believe you love me? Speak again.

ANTONY. Indeed I do. Speak this, and this, and this.
    [Hugging him.]
Thy praises were unjust; but, I'll deserve them,
And yet mend all. Do with me what thou wilt;
Lead me to victory! thou know'st the way.

 VENTIDIUS. And, will you leave this—

ANTONY. Pr'ythee, do not curse her,
And I will leave her; though, Heaven knows, I love
Beyond life, conquest, empire, all, but honour;
But I will leave her.

VENTIDIUS. That's my royal master;
And, shall we fight?

ANTONY. I warrant thee, old soldier.
Thou shalt behold me once again in iron;
And at the head of our old troops, that beat
The Parthians, cry aloud—Come, follow me!

VENTIDIUS. Oh, now I hear my emperor! in that word
Octavius fell. Gods, let me see that day,
And, if I have ten years behind, take all:
I'll thank you for the exchange.

 ANTONY. O Cleopatra!
 VENTIDIUS. Again?

ANTONY. I've done: In that last sigh she went.
Caesar shall know what 'tis to force a lover
From all he holds most dear.

VENTIDIUS. Methinks, you breathe
Another soul: Your looks are more divine;
You speak a hero, and you move a god.

ANTONY. Oh, thou hast fired me; my soul's up in arms,
And mans each part about me: Once again,
That noble eagerness of fight has seized me;
That eagerness with which I darted upward
To Cassius' camp: In vain the steepy hill
Opposed my way; in vain a war of spears
Sung round my head, and planted on my shield;
I won the trenches, while my foremost men
Lagged on the plain below.

VENTIDIUS. Ye gods, ye gods,
For such another honour!

ANTONY. Come on, my soldier!
Our hearts and arms are still the same: I long
Once more to meet our foes; that thou and I,
Like Time and Death, marching before our troops,
May taste fate to them; mow them out a passage,
And, entering where the foremost squadrons yield,
Begin the noble harvest of the field.
    [Exeunt.]

Act II

Scene I

Enter CLEOPATRA, IRAS, and ALEXAS

CLEOPATRA. What shall I do, or whither shall I turn?
Ventidius has o'ercome, and he will go.

ALEXAS. He goes to fight for you.

CLEOPATRA. Then he would see me, ere he went to fight:
Flatter me not: If once he goes, he's lost,
And all my hopes destroyed.

ALEXAS. Does this weak passion
Become a mighty queen?

CLEOPATRA. I am no queen:
Is this to be a queen, to be besieged
By yon insulting Roman, and to wait
Each hour the victor's chain? These ills are small:
For Antony is lost, and I can mourn
For nothing else but him. Now come, Octavius,
I have no more to lose! prepare thy bands;
I'm fit to be a captive: Antony
Has taught my mind the fortune of a slave.

IRAS. Call reason to assist you.

CLEOPATRA. I have none,
And none would have: My love's a noble madness,
Which shows the cause deserved it. Moderate sorrow
Fits vulgar love, and for a vulgar man:
But I have loved with such transcendent passion,
I soared, at first, quite out of reason's view,
And now am lost above it. No, I'm proud
'Tis thus: Would Antony could see me now
Think you he would not sigh, though he must leave me?

Sure he would sigh; for he is noble-natured,
And bears a tender heart: I know him well.
Ah, no, I know him not; I knew him once,
But now 'tis past.

IRAS. Let it be past with you:
Forget him, madam.

CLEOPATRA. Never, never, Iras.
He once was mine; and once, though now 'tis gone,
Leaves a faint image of possession still.

ALEXAS. Think him inconstant, cruel, and ungrateful.

CLEOPATRA. I cannot: If I could, those thoughts were vain.
Faithless, ungrateful, cruel, though he be,
I still must love him.

Enter CHARMION

Now, what news, my Charmion?
Will he be kind? and will he not forsake me?
Am I to live, or die? —nay, do I live?
Or am I dead? for when he gave his answer,
Fate took the word, and then I lived or died.

CHARMION. I found him, madam —

CLEOPATRA. A long speech preparing?
If thou bring'st comfort, haste, and give it me,
For never was more need.

IRAS. I know he loves you.

CLEOPATRA. Had he been kind, her eyes had told me so,
Before her tongue could speak it: Now she studies,
To soften what he said; but give me death,
Just as he sent it, Charmion, undisguised,

And in the words he spoke.

CHARMION. I found him, then,
Encompassed round, I think, with iron statues;
So mute, so motionless his soldiers stood,
While awfully he cast his eyes about,
And every leader's hopes or fears surveyed:
Methought he looked resolved, and yet not pleased.
When he beheld me struggling in the crowd,
He blushed, and bade make way.

ALEXAS. There's comfort yet.

CHARMION. Ventidius fixed his eyes upon my passage
Severely, as he meant to frown me back,
And sullenly gave place: I told my message,
Just as you gave it, broken and disordered;
I numbered in it all your sighs and tears,
And while I moved your pitiful request,
That you but only begged a last farewell,
He fetched an inward groan; and every time
I named you, sighed, as if his heart were breaking,
But, shunned my eyes, and guiltily looked down:
He seemed not now that awful Antony,
Who shook and armed assembly with his nod;
But, making show as he would rub his eyes,
Disguised and blotted out a falling tear.

CLEOPATRA. Did he then weep? And was I worth a tear?
If what thou hast to say be not as pleasing,
Tell me no more, but let me die contented.

CHARMION. He bid me say, — He knew himself so well,
He could deny you nothing, if he saw you;
And therefore—

CLEOPATRA. Thou wouldst say, he would not see me?

CHARMION. And therefore begged you not to use a power,
Which he could ill resist; yet he should ever
Respect you, as he ought.

CLEOPATRA. Is that a word
For Antony to use to Cleopatra?
O that faint word, RESPECT! how I disdain it!
Disdain myself, for loving after it!
He should have kept that word for cold Octavia.
Respect is for a wife: Am I that thing,
That dull, insipid lump, without desires,
And without power to give them?

ALEXAS. You misjudge;
You see through love, and that deludes your sight;
As, what is straight, seems crooked through the water:
But I, who bear my reason undisturbed,
Can see this Antony, this dreaded man,
A fearful slave, who fain would run away,
And shuns his master's eyes: If you pursue him,
My life on't, he still drags a chain along.
That needs must clog his flight.

 CLEOPATRA. Could I believe thee!—

ALEXAS. By every circumstance I know he loves.
True, he's hard prest, by interest and by honour;
Yet he but doubts, and parleys, and casts out
Many a long look for succour.

CLEOPATRA. He sends word,
He fears to see my face.

ALEXAS. And would you more?
He shows his weakness who declines the combat,
And you must urge your fortune. Could he speak
More plainly? To my ears, the message sounds—

Come to my rescue, Cleopatra, come;
Come, free me from Ventidius; from my tyrant:
See me, and give me a pretence to leave him! —
I hear his trumpets. This way he must pass.
Please you, retire a while; I'll work him first,
That he may bend more easy.

CLEOPATRA. You shall rule me;
But all, I fear, in vain.
    [Exit with CHARMION and IRAS.]

ALEXAS. I fear so too;
Though I concealed my thoughts, to make her bold;
But 'tis our utmost means, and fate befriend it!
    [Withdraws.]

    Enter Lictors with Fasces; one bearing the Eagle; then enter
    ANTONY with VENTIDIUS, followed by other Commanders

ANTONY. Octavius is the minion of blind chance,
But holds from virtue nothing.

  VENTIDIUS. Has he courage?

ANTONY. But just enough to season him from coward.
Oh, 'tis the coldest youth upon a charge,
The most deliberate fighter! if he ventures
(As in Illyria once, they say, he did,
To storm a town), 'tis when he cannot choose;
When all the world have fixt their eyes upon him;
And then he lives on that for seven years after;
But, at a close revenge he never fails.

  VENTIDIUS. I heard you challenged him.

ANTONY. I did, Ventidius.
What think'st thou was his answer? 'Twas so tame! —

He said, he had more ways than one to die;
I had not.

VENTIDIUS. Poor!

ANTONY. He has more ways than one;
But he would choose them all before that one.

VENTIDIUS. He first would choose an ague, or a fever.

ANTONY. No; it must be an ague, not a fever;
He Has not warmth enough to die by that.

VENTIDIUS. Or old age and a bed.

ANTONY. Ay, there's his choice,
He would live, like a lamp, to the last wink,
And crawl the utmost verge of life.
O Hercules! Why should a man like this,
Who dares not trust his fate for one great action,
Be all the care of Heaven? Why should he lord it
O'er fourscore thousand men, of whom each one
Is braver than himself?

VENTIDIUS. You conquered for him:
Philippi knows it; there you shared with him
That empire, which your sword made all your own.

ANTONY. Fool that I was, upon my eagle's wings
I bore this wren, till I was tired with soaring,
And now he mounts above me.
Good heavens, is this,—is this the man who braves me?
Who bids my age make way? Drives me before him,
To the world's ridge, and sweeps me off like rubbish?

VENTIDIUS. Sir, we lose time; the troops are mounted all.

ANTONY. Then give the word to march:
I long to leave this prison of a town,
To join thy legions; and, in open field,
Once more to show my face. Lead, my deliverer.

Enter ALEXAS

ALEXAS. Great emperor,
In mighty arms renowned above mankind,
But, in soft pity to the opprest, a god;
This message sends the mournful Cleopatra
To her departing lord.

VENTIDIUS. Smooth sycophant!

ALEXAS. A thousand wishes, and ten thousand prayers,
Millions of blessings wait you to the wars;
Millions of sighs and tears she sends you too,
And would have sent
As many dear embraces to your arms,
As many parting kisses to your lips;
But those, she fears, have wearied you already.

VENTIDIUS. [aside.] False crocodile!

ALEXAS. And yet she begs not now, you would not leave her;
That were a wish too mighty for her hopes,
Too presuming
For her low fortune, and your ebbing love;
That were a wish for her more prosperous days,
Her blooming beauty, and your growing kindness.

ANTONY. [aside.] Well, I must man it out:—What would the
queen?

ALEXAS. First, to these noble warriors, who attend
Your daring courage in the chase of fame,—
Too daring, and too dangerous for her quiet,—
She humbly recommends all she holds dear,

All her own cares and fears, — the care of you.

VENTIDIUS. Yes, witness Actium.

ANTONY. Let him speak, Ventidius.

ALEXAS. You, when his matchless valour bears him forward,
With ardour too heroic, on his foes,
Fall down, as she would do, before his feet;
Lie in his way, and stop the paths of death:
Tell him, this god is not invulnerable;
That absent Cleopatra bleeds in him;
And, that you may remember her petition,
She begs you wear these trifles, as a pawn,
Which, at your wished return, she will redeem
    [Gives jewels to the Commanders.]
With all the wealth of Egypt:
This to the great Ventidius she presents,
Whom she can never count her enemy,
Because he loves her lord.

VENTIDIUS. Tell her, I'll none on't;
I'm not ashamed of honest poverty;
Not all the diamonds of the east can bribe
Ventidius from his faith. I hope to see
These and the rest of all her sparkling store,
Where they shall more deservingly be placed.

ANTONY. And who must wear them then?

VENTIDIUS. The wronged Octavia.

ANTONY. You might have spared that word.

VENTIDIUS. And he that bribe.

ANTONY. But have I no remembrance?

ALEXAS. Yes, a dear one;
Your slave the queen —

ANTONY. My mistress.

ALEXAS. Then your mistress;
Your mistress would, she says, have sent her soul,
But that you had long since; she humbly begs
This ruby bracelet, set with bleeding hearts,
The emblems of her own, may bind your arm.
  [Presenting a bracelet.]

VENTIDIUS. Now, my best lord, — in honour's name, I ask you,
For manhood's sake, and for your own dear safety, —
Touch not these poisoned gifts,
Infected by the sender; touch them not;
Myriads of bluest plagues lie underneath them,
And more than aconite has dipt the silk.

ANTONY. Nay, now you grow too cynical, Ventidius:
A lady's favours may be worn with honour.
What, to refuse her bracelet! On my soul,
When I lie pensive in my tent alone,
'Twill pass the wakeful hours of winter nights,
To tell these pretty beads upon my arm,
To count for every one a soft embrace,
A melting kiss at such and such a time:
And now and then the fury of her love,
When — — And what harm's in this?

ALEXAS. None, none, my lord,
But what's to her, that now 'tis past for ever.

ANTONY. [going to tie it.]
We soldiers are so awkward — help me tie it.

ALEXAS. In faith, my lord, we courtiers too are awkward
In these affairs: so are all men indeed:
Even I, who am not one. But shall I speak?

ANTONY. Yes, freely.

ALEXAS. Then, my lord, fair hands alone
Are fit to tie it; she, who sent it can.

VENTIDIUS. Hell, death! this eunuch pander ruins you.
You will not see her?

[ALEXAS whispers an ATTENDANT, who goes out.]

ANTONY. But to take my leave.

VENTIDIUS. Then I have washed an Aethiop. You're undone;
Y' are in the toils; y' are taken; y' are destroyed:
Her eyes do Caesar's work.

ANTONY. You fear too soon.
I'm constant to myself: I know my strength;
And yet she shall not think me barbarous neither,
Born in the depths of Afric: I am a Roman,
Bred in the rules of soft humanity.
A guest, and kindly used, should bid farewell.

VENTIDIUS. You do not know
How weak you are to her, how much an infant:
You are not proof against a smile, or glance:
A sigh will quite disarm you.

ANTONY. See, she comes!
Now you shall find your error. — Gods, I thank you:
I formed the danger greater than it was,
And now 'tis near, 'tis lessened.

VENTIDIUS. Mark the end yet.

Enter CLEOPATRA, CHARMION, and IRAS

ANTONY. Well, madam, we are met.

CLEOPATRA. Is this a meeting?
Then, we must part?

ANTONY. We must.

CLEOPATRA. Who says we must?

ANTONY. Our own hard fates.

CLEOPATRA. We make those fates ourselves.

ANTONY. Yes, we have made them; we have loved each other,
Into our mutual ruin.

CLEOPATRA. The gods have seen my joys with envious eyes;
I have no friends in heaven; and all the world,
As 'twere the business of mankind to part us,
Is armed against my love: even you yourself
Join with the rest; you, you are armed against me.

ANTONY. I will be justified in all I do
To late posterity, and therefore hear me.
If I mix a lie
With any truth, reproach me freely with it;
Else, favour me with silence.

CLEOPATRA. You command me,
And I am dumb.

VENTIDIUS. I like this well; he shows authority.

ANTONY. That I derive my ruin
From you alone — —

CLEOPATRA. O heavens! I ruin you!

ANTONY. You promised me your silence, and you break it
Ere I have scarce begun.

CLEOPATRA. Well, I obey you.

ANTONY. When I beheld you first, it was in Egypt.
Ere Caesar saw your eyes, you gave me love,
And were too young to know it; that I settled
Your father in his throne, was for your sake;
I left the acknowledgment for time to ripen.
Caesar stept in, and, with a greedy hand,
Plucked the green fruit, ere the first blush of red,
Yet cleaving to the bough. He was my lord,
And was, beside, too great for me to rival;
But, I deserved you first, though he enjoyed you.
When, after, I beheld you in Cilicia,
An enemy to Rome, I pardoned you.

CLEOPATRA. I cleared myself — —

ANTONY. Again you break your promise.
I loved you still, and took your weak excuses,
Took you into my bosom, stained by Caesar,
And not half mine: I went to Egypt with you,
And hid me from the business of the world,
Shut out inquiring nations from my sight,
To give whole years to you.

VENTIDIUS. Yes, to your shame be't spoken.
   [Aside.]

ANTONY. How I loved.
Witness, ye days and nights, and all ye hours,
That danced away with down upon your feet,
As all your business were to count my passion!
One day passed by, and nothing saw but love;
Another came, and still 'twas only love:
The suns were wearied out with looking on,
And I untired with loving.
I saw you every day, and all the day;
And every day was still but as the first,

So eager was I still to see you more.

VENTIDIUS. 'Tis all too true.

ANTONY. Fulvia, my wife, grew jealous,
(As she indeed had reason) raised a war
In Italy, to call me back.

VENTIDIUS. But yet
You went not.

ANTONY. While within your arms I lay,
The world fell mouldering from my hands each hour,
And left me scarce a grasp—I thank your love for't.

VENTIDIUS. Well pushed: that last was home.

CLEOPATRA. Yet may I speak?

ANTONY. If I have urged a falsehood, yes; else, not.
Your silence says, I have not. Fulvia died,
(Pardon, you gods, with my unkindness died);
To set the world at peace, I took Octavia,
This Caesar's sister; in her pride of youth,
And flower of beauty, did I wed that lady,
Whom blushing I must praise, because I left her.
You called; my love obeyed the fatal summons:
This raised the Roman arms; the cause was yours.
I would have fought by land, where I was stronger;
You hindered it: yet, when I fought at sea,
Forsook me fighting; and (O stain to honour!
O lasting shame!) I knew not that I fled;
But fled to follow you.

VENTIDIUS. What haste she made to hoist her purple sails!
And, to appear magnificent in flight,
Drew half our strength away.

ANTONY. All this you caused.
And, would you multiply more ruins on me?
This honest man, my best, my only friend,
Has gathered up the shipwreck of my fortunes;
Twelve legions I have left, my last recruits.
And you have watched the news, and bring your eyes
To seize them too. If you have aught to answer,
Now speak, you have free leave.

ALEXAS. [aside.] She stands confounded:
Despair is in her eyes.

VENTIDIUS. Now lay a sigh in the way to stop his passage:
Prepare a tear, and bid it for his legions;
'Tis like they shall be sold.

CLEOPATRA. How shall I plead my cause, when you, my judge,
Already have condemned me? Shall I bring
The love you bore me for my advocate?
That now is turned against me, that destroys me;
For love, once past, is, at the best, forgotten;
But oftener sours to hate: 'twill please my lord
To ruin me, and therefore I'll be guilty.
But, could I once have thought it would have pleased you,
That you would pry, with narrow searching eyes,
Into my faults, severe to my destruction,
And watching all advantages with care,
That serve to make me wretched? Speak, my lord,
For I end here. Though I deserved this usage,
Was it like you to give it?

ANTONY. Oh, you wrong me,
To think I sought this parting, or desired
To accuse you more than what will clear myself,
And justify this breach.

CLEOPATRA. Thus low I thank you;
And, since my innocence will not offend,
I shall not blush to own it.

VENTIDIUS. After this,
I think she'll blush at nothing.

CLEOPATRA. You seem grieved
(And therein you are kind) that Caesar first
Enjoyed my love, though you deserved it better:
I grieve for that, my lord, much more than you;
For, had I first been yours, it would have saved
My second choice: I never had been his,
And ne'er had been but yours. But Caesar first,
You say, possessed my love. Not so, my lord:
He first possessed my person; you, my love:
Caesar loved me; but I loved Antony.
If I endured him after, 'twas because
I judged it due to the first name of men;
And, half constrained, I gave, as to a tyrant,
What he would take by force.

VENTIDIUS. O Syren! Syren!
Yet grant that all the love she boasts were true,
Has she not ruined you? I still urge that,
The fatal consequence.

CLEOPATRA. The consequence indeed —
For I dare challenge him, my greatest foe,
To say it was designed: 'tis true, I loved you,
And kept you far from an uneasy wife, —
Such Fulvia was.
Yes, but he'll say, you left Octavia for me; —
And, can you blame me to receive that love,
Which quitted such desert, for worthless me?
How often have I wished some other Caesar,
Great as the first, and as the second young,

Would court my love, to be refused for you!

 VENTIDIUS. Words, words; but Actium, sir; remember Actium.

CLEOPATRA. Even there, I dare his malice. True, I counselled
To fight at sea; but I betrayed you not.
I fled, but not to the enemy. 'Twas fear;
Would I had been a man, not to have feared!
For none would then have envied me your friendship,
Who envy me your love.

ANTONY. We are both unhappy:
If nothing else, yet our ill fortune parts us.
Speak; would you have me perish by my stay?

CLEOPATRA. If, as a friend, you ask my judgment, go;
If, as a lover, stay. If you must perish—
'Tis a hard word—but stay.

VENTIDIUS. See now the effects of her so boasted love!
She strives to drag you down to ruin with her;
But, could she 'scape without you, oh, how soon
Would she let go her hold, and haste to shore,
And never look behind!

CLEOPATRA. Then judge my love by this.
    [Giving ANTONY a writing.]
Could I have borne
A life or death, a happiness or woe,
From yours divided, this had given me means.

ANTONY. By Hercules, the writing of Octavius!
I know it well: 'tis that proscribing hand,
Young as it was, that led the way to mine,
And left me but the second place in murder.—
See, see, Ventidius! here he offers Egypt,

And joins all Syria to it, as a present;
So, in requital, she forsake my fortunes,
And join her arms with his.

CLEOPATRA. And yet you leave me!
You leave me, Antony; and yet I love you,
Indeed I do: I have refused a kingdom;
That is a trifle;
For I could part with life, with anything,
But only you. Oh, let me die but with you!
Is that a hard request?

ANTONY. Next living with you,
'Tis all that Heaven can give.

ALEXAS. He melts; we conquer.
    [Aside.]

CLEOPATRA. No; you shall go: your interest calls you hence;
Yes; your dear interest pulls too strong, for these
Weak arms to hold you here.
    [Takes his hand.]
Go; leave me, soldier
(For you're no more a lover): leave me dying:
Push me, all pale and panting, from your bosom,
And, when your march begins, let one run after,
Breathless almost for joy, and cry—She's dead.
The soldiers shout; you then, perhaps, may sigh,
And muster all your Roman gravity:
Ventidius chides; and straight your brow clears up,
As I had never been.

  ANTONY. Gods, 'tis too much; too much for man to bear.

CLEOPATRA. What is't for me then,
A weak, forsaken woman, and a lover?—
Here let me breathe my last: envy me not

This minute in your arms: I'll die apace,
As fast as e'er I can, and end your trouble.

ANTONY. Die! rather let me perish; loosened nature
Leap from its hinges, sink the props of heaven,
And fall the skies, to crush the nether world!
My eyes, my soul, my all!
    [Embraces her.]

VENTIDIUS. And what's this toy,
In balance with your fortune, honour, fame?

ANTONY. What is't, Ventidius? — it outweighs them all;
Why, we have more than conquered Caesar now:
My queen's not only innocent, but loves me.
This, this is she, who drags me down to ruin!
"But, could she 'scape without me, with what haste
Would she let slip her hold, and make to shore,
And never look behind!"
Down on thy knees, blasphemer as thou art,
And ask forgiveness of wronged innocence.

 VENTIDIUS. I'll rather die, than take it. Will you go?

ANTONY. Go! whither? Go from all that's excellent?
Faith, honour, virtue, all good things forbid,
That I should go from her, who sets my love
Above the price of kingdoms! Give, you gods,
Give to your boy, your Caesar,
This rattle of a globe to play withal,
This gewgaw world, and put him cheaply off:
I'll not be pleased with less than Cleopatra.

CLEOPATRA. She's wholly yours. My heart's so full of joy,
That I shall do some wild extravagance
Of love, in public; and the foolish world,

Which knows not tenderness, will think me mad.

VENTIDIUS. O women! women! women! all the gods
Have not such power of doing good to man,
As you of doing harm.
    [Exit.]

ANTONY. Our men are armed: —
Unbar the gate that looks to Caesar's camp:
I would revenge the treachery he meant me;
And long security makes conquest easy.
I'm eager to return before I go;
For, all the pleasures I have known beat thick
On my remembrance. — How I long for night!
That both the sweets of mutual love may try,
And triumph once o'er Caesar ere we die.
    [Exeunt.]

Act III

Scene I

At one door enter CLEOPATRA, CHARMION, IRAS, and
ALEXAS, a Train of EGYPTIANS: at the other ANTONY and RO-
MANS. The entrance on both sides is prepared by music; the trumpets first sounding on Antony's part: then answered by timbrels,
etc., on CLEOPATRA'S. CHARMION and IRAS hold a laurel
wreath betwixt them. A Dance of EGYPTIANS. After the ceremony,
CLEOPATRA crowns ANTONY.

ANTONY. I thought how those white arms would fold me in,
And strain me close, and melt me into love;
So pleased with that sweet image, I sprung forwards,
And added all my strength to every blow.

CLEOPATRA. Come to me, come, my soldier, to my arms!
You've been too long away from my embraces;
But, when I have you fast, and all my own,
With broken murmurs, and with amorous sighs,
I'll say, you were unkind, and punish you,
And mark you red with many an eager kiss.

ANTONY. My brighter Venus!

CLEOPATRA. O my greater Mars!

ANTONY. Thou join'st us well, my love!
Suppose me come from the Phlegraean plains,
Where gasping giants lay, cleft by my sword,
And mountain-tops paired off each other blow,
To bury those I slew. Receive me, goddess!
Let Caesar spread his subtle nets; like Vulcan,
In thy embraces I would be beheld
By heaven and earth at once;
And make their envy what they meant their sport
Let those, who took us, blush; I would love on,
With awful state, regardless of their frowns,
As their superior gods.
There's no satiety of love in thee:
Enjoyed, thou still art new; perpetual spring
Is in thy arms; the ripened fruit but falls,
And blossoms rise to fill its empty place;
And I grow rich by giving.

Enter VENTIDIUS, and stands apart

ALEXAS. Oh, now the danger's past, your general comes!
He joins not in your joys, nor minds your triumphs;
But, with contracted brows, looks frowning on,
As envying your success.

ANTONY. Now, on my soul, he loves me; truly loves me:
He never flattered me in any vice,
But awes me with his virtue: even this minute,

Methinks, he has a right of chiding me.
Lead to the temple: I'll avoid his presence;
It checks too strong upon me.
    [Exeunt the rest.]
    [As ANTONY is going, VENTIDIUS pulls him by the robe.]

  VENTIDIUS. Emperor!

ANTONY. 'Tis the old argument; I pr'ythee, spare me.
    [Looking back.]

  VENTIDIUS. But this one hearing, emperor.

ANTONY. Let go
My robe; or, by my father Hercules —

VENTIDIUS. By Hercules' father, that's yet greater,
I bring you somewhat you would wish to know.

ANTONY. Thou see'st we are observed; attend me here,
And I'll return.
    [Exit.]

VENTIDIUS. I am waning in his favour, yet I love him;
I love this man, who runs to meet his ruin;
And sure the gods, like me, are fond of him:
His virtues lie so mingled with his crimes,
As would confound their choice to punish one,
And not reward the other.

  Enter ANTONY

ANTONY. We can conquer,
You see, without your aid.
We have dislodged their troops;
They look on us at distance, and, like curs
Scaped from the lion's paws, they bay far off,

And lick their wounds, and faintly threaten war.
Five thousand Romans, with their faces upward,
Lie breathless on the plain.

VENTIDIUS. 'Tis well; and he,
Who lost them, could have spared ten thousand more.
Yet if, by this advantage, you could gain
An easier peace, while Caesar doubts the chance
Of arms—

ANTONY. Oh, think not on't, Ventidius!
The boy pursues my ruin, he'll no peace;
His malice is considerable in advantage.
Oh, he's the coolest murderer! so staunch,
He kills, and keeps his temper.

VENTIDIUS. Have you no friend
In all his army, who has power to move him?
Maecenas, or Agrippa, might do much.

ANTONY. They're both too deep in Caesar's interests.
We'll work it out by dint of sword, or perish.

VENTIDIUS. Fain I would find some other.

ANTONY. Thank thy love.
Some four or five such victories as this
Will save thy further pains.

VENTIDIUS. Expect no more; Caesar is on his guard:
I know, sir, you have conquered against odds;
But still you draw supplies from one poor town,
And of Egyptians: he has all the world,
And, at his beck, nations come pouring in,
To fill the gaps you make. Pray, think again.

ANTONY. Why dost thou drive me from myself, to search
For foreign aids?—to hunt my memory,
And range all o'er a waste and barren place,
To find a friend? The wretched have no friends.
Yet I had one, the bravest youth of Rome,
Whom Caesar loves beyond the love of women:
He could resolve his mind, as fire does wax,
From that hard rugged image melt him down,
And mould him in what softer form he pleased.

VENTIDIUS. Him would I see; that man, of all the world;
Just such a one we want.

ANTONY. He loved me too;
I was his soul; he lived not but in me:
We were so closed within each other's breasts,
The rivets were not found, that joined us first.
That does not reach us yet: we were so mixt,
As meeting streams, both to ourselves were lost;
We were one mass; we could not give or take,
But from the same; for he was I, I he.

VENTIDIUS. He moves as I would wish him.
  [Aside.]

ANTONY. After this,
I need not tell his name;—'twas Dolabella.

VENTIDIUS. He's now in Caesar's camp.

ANTONY. No matter where,
Since he's no longer mine. He took unkindly,
That I forbade him Cleopatra's sight,
Because I feared he loved her: he confessed,
He had a warmth, which, for my sake, he stifled;
For 'twere impossible that two, so one,
Should not have loved the same. When he departed,

He took no leave; and that confirmed my thoughts.

VENTIDIUS. It argues, that he loved you more than her,
Else he had stayed; but he perceived you jealous,
And would not grieve his friend: I know he loves you.

ANTONY. I should have seen him, then, ere now.

VENTIDIUS. Perhaps
He has thus long been labouring for your peace.

ANTONY. Would he were here!

VENTIDIUS. Would you believe he loved you?
I read your answer in your eyes, you would.
Not to conceal it longer, he has sent
A messenger from Caesar's camp, with letters.

ANTONY. Let him appear.

VENTIDIUS. I'll bring him instantly.
    [Exit VENTIDIUS, and re-enters immediately with DOLABEL-
LA.]

ANTONY. 'Tis he himself! himself, by holy friendship!
    [Runs to embrace him.]
Art thou returned at last, my better half?
Come, give me all myself!
Let me not live,
If the young bridegroom, longing for his night,
Was ever half so fond.

DOLABELLA. I must be silent, for my soul is busy
About a nobler work; she's new come home,
Like a long-absent man, and wanders o'er
Each room, a stranger to her own, to look

If all be safe.

ANTONY. Thou hast what's left of me;
For I am now so sunk from what I was,
Thou find'st me at my lowest water-mark.
The rivers that ran in, and raised my fortunes,
Are all dried up, or take another course:
What I have left is from my native spring;
I've still a heart that swells, in scorn of fate,
And lifts me to my banks.

DOLABELLA. Still you are lord of all the world to me.

ANTONY. Why, then I yet am so; for thou art all.
If I had any joy when thou wert absent,
I grudged it to myself; methought I robbed
Thee of thy part. But, O my Dolabella!
Thou has beheld me other than I am.
Hast thou not seen my morning chambers filled
With sceptred slaves, who waited to salute me?
With eastern monarchs, who forgot the sun,
To worship my uprising? — menial kings
Ran coursing up and down my palace-yard,
Stood silent in my presence, watched my eyes,
And, at my least command, all started out,
Like racers to the goal.

DOLABELLA. Slaves to your fortune.

ANTONY. Fortune is Caesar's now; and what am I?

VENTIDIUS. What you have made yourself; I will not flatter.

ANTONY. Is this friendly done?

DOLABELLA. Yes; when his end is so, I must join with him;
Indeed I must, and yet you must not chide;
Why am I else your friend?

ANTONY. Take heed, young man,
How thou upbraid'st my love: The queen has eyes,
And thou too hast a soul. Canst thou remember,
When, swelled with hatred, thou beheld'st her first,
As accessary to thy brother's death?

DOLABELLA. Spare my remembrance; 'twas a guilty day,
And still the blush hangs here.

ANTONY. To clear herself,
For sending him no aid, she came from Egypt.
Her galley down the silver Cydnus rowed,
The tackling silk, the streamers waved with gold;
The gentle winds were lodged in purple sails:
Her nymphs, like Nereids, round her couch were placed;
Where she, another sea-born Venus, lay.

DOLABELLA. No more; I would not hear it.

ANTONY. Oh, you must!
She lay, and leant her cheek upon her hand,
And cast a look so languishingly sweet,
As if, secure of all beholders' hearts,
Neglecting, she could take them: boys, like Cupids,
Stood fanning, with their painted wings, the winds.
That played about her face. But if she smiled
A darting glory seemed to blaze abroad,
That men's desiring eyes were never wearied,
But hung upon the object: To soft flutes
The silver oars kept time; and while they played,
The hearing gave new pleasure to the sight;
And both to thought. 'Twas heaven, or somewhat more;
For she so charmed all hearts, that gazing crowds
Stood panting on the shore, and wanted breath
To give their welcome voice.
Then, Dolabella, where was then thy soul?
Was not thy fury quite disarmed with wonder?
Didst thou not shrink behind me from those eyes

And whisper in my ear—Oh, tell her not
That I accused her with my brother's death?

DOLABELLA. And should my weakness be a plea for yours?
Mine was an age when love might be excused,
When kindly warmth, and when my springing youth
Made it a debt to nature. Yours—

VENTIDIUS. Speak boldly.
Yours, he would say, in your declining age,
When no more heat was left but what you forced,
When all the sap was needful for the trunk,
When it went down, then you constrained the course,
And robbed from nature, to supply desire;
In you (I would not use so harsh a word)
'Tis but plain dotage.

ANTONY. Ha!

DOLABELLA. 'Twas urged too home.—
But yet the loss was private, that I made;
'Twas but myself I lost: I lost no legions;
I had no world to lose, no people's love.

ANTONY. This from a friend?

DOLABELLA. Yes, Antony, a true one;
A friend so tender, that each word I speak
Stabs my own heart, before it reach your ear.
Oh, judge me not less kind, because I chide!
To Caesar I excuse you.

ANTONY. O ye gods!
Have I then lived to be excused to Caesar?

DOLABELLA. As to your equal.

ANTONY. Well, he's but my equal:
While I wear this he never shall be more.

 DOLABELLA. I bring conditions from him.

ANTONY. Are they noble?
Methinks thou shouldst not bring them else; yet he
Is full of deep dissembling; knows no honour
Divided from his interest. Fate mistook him;
For nature meant him for an usurer:
He's fit indeed to buy, not conquer kingdoms.

VENTIDIUS. Then, granting this,
What power was theirs, who wrought so hard a temper
To honourable terms?

 ANTONY. I was my Dolabella, or some god.

DOLABELLA. Nor I, nor yet Maecenas, nor Agrippa:
They were your enemies; and I, a friend,
Too weak alone; yet 'twas a Roman's deed.

ANTONY. 'Twas like a Roman done: show me that man,
Who has preserved my life, my love, my honour;
Let me but see his face.

VENTIDIUS. That task is mine,
And, Heaven, thou know'st how pleasing.
    [Exit VENTIDIUS.]

DOLABELLA. You'll remember
To whom you stand obliged?

ANTONY. When I forget it
Be thou unkind, and that's my greatest curse.

My queen shall thank him too,

DOLABELLA. I fear she will not.

ANTONY. But she shall do it: The queen, my Dolabella!
Hast thou not still some grudgings of thy fever?

DOLABELLA. I would not see her lost.

ANTONY. When I forsake her,
Leave me my better stars! for she has truth
Beyond her beauty. Caesar tempted her,
At no less price than kingdoms, to betray me;
But she resisted all: and yet thou chidest me
For loving her too well. Could I do so?

DOLABELLA. Yes; there's my reason.

Re-enter VENTIDIUS, with OCTAVIA,
leading ANTONY'S two little DAUGHTERS

ANTONY. Where?—Octavia there!
[Starting back.]

VENTIDIUS. What, is she poison to you?—a disease?
Look on her, view her well, and those she brings:
Are they all strangers to your eyes? has nature
No secret call, no whisper they are yours?

DOLABELLA. For shame, my lord, if not for love, receive them
With kinder eyes. If you confess a man,
Meet them, embrace them, bid them welcome to you.
Your arms should open, even without your knowledge,
To clasp them in; your feet should turn to wings,
To bear you to them; and your eyes dart out
And aim a kiss, ere you could reach the lips.

ANTONY. I stood amazed, to think how they came hither.

VENTIDIUS. I sent for them; I brought them in unknown
To Cleopatra's guards.

DOLABELLA. Yet, are you cold?

OCTAVIA. Thus long I have attended for my welcome;
Which, as a stranger, sure I might expect.
Who am I?

ANTONY. Caesar's sister.

OCTAVIA. That's unkind.
Had I been nothing more than Caesar's sister,
Know, I had still remained in Caesar's camp:
But your Octavia, your much injured wife,
Though banished from your bed, driven from your house,
In spite of Caesar's sister, still is yours.
'Tis true, I have a heart disdains your coldness,
And prompts me not to seek what you should offer;
But a wife's virtue still surmounts that pride.
I come to claim you as my own; to show
My duty first; to ask, nay beg, your kindness:
Your hand, my lord; 'tis mine, and I will have it.
    [Taking his hand.]

VENTIDIUS. Do, take it; thou deserv'st it.

DOLABELLA. On my soul,
And so she does: she's neither too submissive,
Nor yet too haughty; but so just a mean
Shows, as it ought, a wife and Roman too.

ANTONY. I fear, Octavia, you have begged my life.

OCTAVIA. Begged it, my lord?

ANTONY. Yes, begged it, my ambassadress;
Poorly and basely begged it of your brother.

OCTAVIA. Poorly and basely I could never beg:
Nor could my brother grant.

ANTONY. Shall I, who, to my kneeling slave, could say,
Rise up, and be a king; shall I fall down
And cry, — Forgive me, Caesar! Shall I set
A man, my equal, in the place of Jove,
As he could give me being? No; that word,
Forgive, would choke me up,
And die upon my tongue.

DOLABELLA. You shall not need it.

ANTONY. I will not need it. Come, you've all betrayed me, —
My friend too! — to receiv e some vile conditions.
My wife has bought me, with her prayers and tears;
And now I must become her branded slave.
In every peevish mood, she will upbraid
The life she gave: if I but look awry,
She cries — I'll tell my brother.

OCTAVIA. My hard fortune
Subjects me still to your unkind mistakes.
But the conditions I have brought are such,
Your need not blush to take: I love your honour,
Because 'tis mine; it never shall be said,
Octavia's husband was her brother's slave.
Sir, you are free; free, even from her you loathe;
For, though my brother bargains for your love,
Makes me the price and cement of your peace,
I have a soul like yours; I cannot take
Your love as alms, nor beg what I deserve.
I'll tell my brother we are reconciled;
He shall draw back his troops, and you shall march

To rule the East: I may be dropt at Athens;
No matter where. I never will complain,
But only keep the barren name of wife,
And rid you of the trouble.

VENTIDIUS. Was ever such a strife of sullen honour! [Apart]
Both scorn to be obliged.

DOLABELLA. Oh, she has touched him in the tenderest
part;[Apart]
 See how he reddens with despite and shame,
 To be outdone in generosity!

VENTIDIUS. See how he winks! how he dries up a tear, [Apart]
That fain would fall!

ANTONY. Octavia, I have heard you, and must praise
The greatness of your soul;
But cannot yield to what you have proposed:
For I can ne'er be conquered but by love;
And you do all for duty. You would free me,
And would be dropt at Athens; was't not so?

 OCTAVIA. It was, my lord.

ANTONY. Then I must be obliged
To one who loves me not; who, to herself,
May call me thankless and ungrateful man: —
I'll not endure it; no.

VENTIDIUS. I am glad it pinches there.
    [Aside.]

OCTAVIA. Would you triumph o'er poor Octavia's virtue?
That pride was all I had to bear me up;
That you might think you owed me for your life,

And owed it to my duty, not my love.
I have been injured, and my haughty soul
Could brook but ill the man who slights my bed.

ANTONY. Therefore you love me not.

OCTAVIA. Therefore, my lord,
I should not love you.

ANTONY. Therefore you would leave me?

OCTAVIA. And therefore I should leave you—if I could.

DOLABELLA. Her soul's too great, after such injuries,
To say she loves; and yet she lets you see it.
Her modesty and silence plead her cause.

ANTONY. O Dolabella, which way shall I turn?
I find a secret yielding in my soul;
But Cleopatra, who would die with me,
Must she be left? Pity pleads for Octavia;
But does it not plead more for Cleopatra?

VENTIDIUS. Justice and pity both plead for Octavia;
For Cleopatra, neither.
One would be ruined with you; but she first
Had ruined you: The other, you have ruined,
And yet she would preserve you.
In everything their merits are unequal.

ANTONY. O my distracted soul!

OCTAVIA. Sweet Heaven compose it!—
Come, come, my lord, if I can pardon you,
Methinks you should accept it. Look on these;
Are they not yours? or stand they thus neglected,
As they are mine? Go to him, children, go;
Kneel to him, take him by the hand, speak to him;
For you may speak, and he may own you too,

Without a blush; and so he cannot all
His children: go, I say, and pull him to me,
And pull him to yourselves, from that bad woman.
You, Agrippina, hang upon his arms;
And you, Antonia, clasp about his waist:
If he will shake you off, if he will dash you
Against the pavement, you must bear it, children;
For you are mine, and I was born to suffer.
  [Here the CHILDREN go to him, etc.]

VENTIDIUS. Was ever sight so moving? — Emperor!

DOLABELLA. Friend!

OCTAVIA. Husband!

BOTH CHILDREN. Father!

ANTONY. I am vanquished: take me,
Octavia; take me, children; share me all.
  [Embracing them.]

I've been a thriftless debtor to your loves,
And run out much, in riot, from your stock;
But all shall be amended.

OCTAVIA. O blest hour!

DOLABELLA. O happy change!

VENTIDIUS. My joy stops at my tongue;
But it has found two channels here for one,
And bubbles out above.

ANTONY. [to OCTAVIA]
This is thy triumph; lead me where thou wilt;
Even to thy brother's camp.

OCTAVIA. All there are yours.

Enter ALEXAS hastily

ALEXAS. The queen, my mistress, sir, and yours—

ANTONY. 'Tis past.—
Octavia, you shall stay this night: To-morrow,
Caesar and we are one.
    [Exit leading OCTAVIA; DOLABELLA and the CHILDREN
follow.]

VENTIDIUS. There's news for you; run, my officious eunuch,
Be sure to be the first; haste forward:
Haste, my dear eunuch, haste.
    [Exit.]

ALEXAS. This downright fighting fool, this thick-skulled hero,
This blunt, unthinking instrument of death,
With plain dull virtue has outgone my wit.
Pleasure forsook my earliest infancy;
The luxury of others robbed my cradle,
And ravished thence the promise of a man.
Cast out from nature, disinherited
Of what her meanest children claim by kind,
Yet greatness kept me from contempt: that's gone.
Had Cleopatra followed my advice,
Then he had been betrayed who now forsakes.
She dies for love; but she has known its joys:
Gods, is this just, that I, who know no joys,
Must die, because she loves?

Enter CLEOPATRA, CHARMION, IRAS, and Train

O madam, I have seen what blasts my eyes!
Octavia's here.

CLEOPATRA. Peace with that raven's note.
I know it too; and now am in

The pangs of death.

ALEXAS. You are no more a queen;
Egypt is lost.

CLEOPATRA. What tell'st thou me of Egypt?
My life, my soul is lost! Octavia has him!—
O fatal name to Cleopatra's love!
My kisses, my embraces now are hers;
While I—But thou hast seen my rival; speak,
Does she deserve this blessing? Is she fair?
Bright as a goddess? and is all perfection
Confined to her? It is. Poor I was made
Of that coarse matter, which, when she was finished,
The gods threw by for rubbish.

ALEXAS. She is indeed a very miracle.

CLEOPATRA. Death to my hopes, a miracle!

ALEXAS. A miracle;
    [Bowing.]
I mean of goodness; for in beauty, madam,
You make all wonders cease.

CLEOPATRA. I was too rash:
Take this in part of recompense. But, oh!
    [Giving a ring.]
I fear thou flatterest me.

CHARMION. She comes! she's here!

IRAS. Fly, madam, Caesar's sister!

CLEOPATRA. Were she the sister of the thunderer Jove,
And bore her brother's lightning in her eyes,
Thus would I face my rival.
    [Meets OCTAVIA with VENTIDIUS. OCTAVIA bears up

to her. Their Trains come up on either side.]

OCTAVIA. I need not ask if you are Cleopatra;
Your haughty carriage —

CLEOPATRA. Shows I am a queen:
Nor need I ask you, who you are.

OCTAVIA. A Roman:
A name, that makes and can unmake a queen.

  CLEOPATRA. Your lord, the man who serves me, is a Roman.

OCTAVIA. He was a Roman, till he lost that name,
To be a slave in Egypt; but I come
To free him thence.

CLEOPATRA. Peace, peace, my lover's Juno.
When he grew weary of that household clog,
He chose my easier bonds.

OCTAVIA. I wonder not
Your bonds are easy: you have long been practised
In that lascivious art: He's not the first
 For whom you spread your snares: Let Caesar witness.

CLEOPATRA. I loved not Caesar; 'twas but gratitude
I paid his love: The worst your malice can,
Is but to say the greatest of mankind
Has been my slave. The next, but far above him
In my esteem, is he whom law calls yours,
But whom his love made mine.

OCTAVIA. I would view nearer.
   [Coming up close to her.]

That face, which has so long usurped my right,
To find the inevitable charms, that catch
Mankind so sure, that ruined my dear lord.

CLEOPATRA. Oh, you do well to search; for had you known
But half these charms, you had not lost his heart.

OCTAVIA. Far be their knowledge from a Roman lady,
Far from a modest wife! Shame of our sex,
Dost thou not blush to own those black endearments,
That make sin pleasing?

CLEOPATRA. You may blush, who want them.
If bounteous nature, if indulgent Heaven
Have given me charms to please the bravest man,
Should I not thank them? Should I be ashamed,
And not be proud? I am, that he has loved me;
And, when I love not him, Heaven change this face
For one like that.

 OCTAVIA. Thou lov'st him not so well.

 CLEOPATRA. I love him better, and deserve him more.

OCTAVIA. You do not; cannot: You have been his ruin.
Who made him cheap at Rome, but Cleopatra?
Who made him scorned abroad, but Cleopatra?
At Actium, who betrayed him? Cleopatra.
Who made his children orphans, and poor me
A wretched widow? only Cleopatra.

CLEOPATRA. Yet she, who loves him best, is Cleopatra.
If you have suffered, I have suffered more.
You bear the specious title of a wife,
To gild your cause, and draw the pitying world
To favour it: the world condemns poor me.
For I have lost my honour, lost my fame,

And stained the glory of my royal house,
And all to bear the branded name of mistress.
There wants but life, and that too I would lose
For him I love.

OCTAVIA. Be't so, then; take thy wish.
  [Exit with her Train.]

CLEOPATRA. And 'tis my wish,
Now he is lost for whom alone I lived.
My sight grows dim, and every object dances,
And swims before me, in the maze of death.
My spirits, while they were opposed, kept up;
They could not sink beneath a rival's scorn!
But now she's gone, they faint.

ALEXAS. Mine have had leisure
To recollect their strength, and furnish counsel,
To ruin her, who else must ruin you.

CLEOPATRA. Vain promiser!
Lead me, my Charmion; nay, your hand too, Iras.
My grief has weight enough to sink you both.
Conduct me to some solitary chamber,
And draw the curtains round;
Then leave me to myself, to take alone
My fill of grief:
  There I till death will his unkindness weep;
  As harmless infants moan themselves asleep.
    [Exeunt.]

Act IV

Scene I

Enter ANTONY and DOLABELLA

DOLABELLA. Why would you shift it from yourself on me?
Can you not tell her, you must part?

ANTONY. I cannot.
I could pull out an eye, and bid it go,
And t'other should not weep. O Dolabella,
How many deaths are in this word, DEPART!
I dare not trust my tongue to tell her so:
One look of hers would thaw me into tears,
And I should melt, till I were lost again.

DOLABELLA. Then let Ventidius;
He's rough by nature.

ANTONY. Oh, he'll speak too harshly;
He'll kill her with the news: Thou, only thou.

DOLABELLA. Nature has cast me in so soft a mould,
That but to hear a story, feigned for pleasure,
Of some sad lover's death, moistens my eyes,
And robs me of my manhood. I should speak
So faintly, with such fear to grieve her heart,
She'd not believe it earnest.

ANTONY. Therefore, — therefore
Thou only, thou art fit: Think thyself me;
And when thou speak'st (but let it first be long),
Take off the edge from every sharper sound,
And let our parting be as gently made,
As other loves begin: Wilt thou do this?

DOLABELLA. What you have said so sinks into my soul,
That, if I must speak, I shall speak just so.

ANTONY. I leave you then to your sad task: Farewell.
I sent her word to meet you.
　　[Goes to the door, and comes back.]
I forgot;
Let her be told, I'll make her peace with mine,
Her crown and dignity shall be preserved,
If I have power with Caesar. — Oh, be sure
To think on that.

DOLABELLA. Fear not, I will remember.
　　[ANTONY goes again to the door, and comes back.]

ANTONY. And tell her, too, how much I was constrained;
I did not this, but with extremest force.
Desire her not to hate my memory,
For I still cherish hers: — insist on that.

　DOLABELLA. Trust me. I'll not forget it.

ANTONY. Then that's all.
　　[Goes out, and returns again.]
Wilt thou forgive my fondness this once more?
Tell her, though we shall never meet again,
If I should hear she took another love,
The news would break my heart. — Now I must go;
For every time I have returned, I feel
My soul more tender; and my next command
Would be, to bid her stay, and ruin both.
　　[Exit.]

DOLABELLA. Men are but children of a larger growth;
Our appetites as apt to change as theirs,
And full as craving too, and full as vain;
And yet the soul, shut up in her dark room,

Viewing so clear abroad, at home sees nothing:
But, like a mole in earth, busy and blind,
Works all her folly up, and casts it outward
To the world's open view: Thus I discovered,
And blamed the love of ruined Antony:
Yet wish that I were he, to be so ruined.

  Enter VENTIDIUS above

VENTIDIUS. Alone, and talking to himself? concerned too?
Perhaps my guess is right; he loved her once,
And may pursue it still.

DOLABELLA. O friendship! friendship!
Ill canst thou answer this; and reason, worse:
Unfaithful in the attempt; hopeless to win;
And if I win, undone: mere madness all.
And yet the occasion's fair. What injury
To him, to wear the robe which he throws by!

VENTIDIUS. None, none at all. This happens as I wish,
To ruin her yet more with Antony.

  Enter CLEOPATRA talking with ALEXAS;
  CHARMION, IRAS on the other side.

DOLABELLA. She comes! What charms have sorrow on that face!
Sorrow seems pleased to dwell with so much sweetness;
Yet, now and then, a melancholy smile
Breaks loose, like lightning in a winter's night,
And shows a moment's day.

VENTIDIUS. If she should love him too! her eunuch there?
That porc'pisce bodes ill weather. Draw, draw nearer,
Sweet devil, that I may hear.

ALEXAS. Believe me; try

    [DOLABELLA goes over to CHARMION and IRAS;
    seems to talk with them.]

To make him jealous; jealousy is like
A polished glass held to the lips when life's in doubt;
If there be breath, 'twill catch the damp, and show it.

CLEOPATRA. I grant you, jealousy's a proof of love,
But 'tis a weak and unavailing medicine;
It puts out the disease, and makes it show,
But has no power to cure.

ALEXAS. 'Tis your last remedy, and strongest too:
And then this Dolabella, who so fit
To practise on? He's handsome, valiant, young,
And looks as he were laid for nature's bait,
To catch weak women's eyes.
He stands already more than half suspected
Of loving you: the least kind word or glance,
You give this youth, will kindle him with love:
Then, like a burning vessel set adrift,
You'll send him down amain before the wind,
To fire the heart of jealous Antony.

CLEOPATRA. Can I do this? Ah, no, my love's so true,
That I can neither hide it where it is,
Nor show it where it is not. Nature meant me
A wife; a silly, harmless, household dove,
Fond without art, and kind without deceit;
But Fortune, that has made a mistress of me,
Has thrust me out to the wide world, unfurnished
Of falsehood to be happy.

ALEXAS. Force yourself.
The event will be, your lover will return,
Doubly desirous to possess the good

Which once he feared to lose.

CLEOPATRA. I must attempt it;
But oh, with what regret!
   [Exit ALEXAS. She comes up to DOLABELLA.]

 VENTIDIUS. So, now the scene draws near; they're in my reach.

CLEOPATRA. [to DOLABELLA.]
Discoursing with my women! might not I
Share in your entertainment?

CHARMION. You have been
The subject of it, madam.

 CLEOPATRA. How! and how!

 IRAS. Such praises of your beauty!

CLEOPATRA. Mere poetry.
Your Roman wits, your Gallus and Tibullus,
Have taught you this from Cytheris and Delia.

DOLABELLA. Those Roman wits have never been in Egypt;
Cytheris and Delia else had been unsung:
I, who have seen—had I been born a poet,
Should choose a nobler name.

CLEOPATRA. You flatter me.
But, 'tis your nation's vice: All of your country
Are flatterers, and all false. Your friend's like you.
I'm sure, he sent you not to speak these words.

 DOLABELLA. No, madam; yet he sent me—

 CLEOPATRA. Well, he sent you—

 DOLABELLA. Of a less pleasing errand.

CLEOPATRA. How less pleasing?
Less to yourself, or me?

DOLABELLA. Madam, to both;
For you must mourn, and I must grieve to cause it.

CLEOPATRA. You, Charmion, and your fellow, stand at distance. —
Hold up, my spirits. [Aside.] — Well, now your mournful matter;
For I'm prepared, perhaps can guess it too.

DOLABELLA. I wish you would; for 'tis a thankless office,
To tell ill news: And I, of all your sex,
Most fear displeasing you.

CLEOPATRA. Of all your sex,
I soonest could forgive you, if you should.

VENTIDIUS. Most delicate advances! Women! women!
Dear, damned, inconstant sex!

CLEOPATRA. In the first place,
I am to be forsaken; is't not so?

DOLABELLA. I wish I could not answer to that question.

CLEOPATRA. Then pass it o'er, because it troubles you:
I should have been more grieved another time.
Next I'm to lose my kingdom — Farewell, Egypt!
Yet, is there ary more?

DOLABELLA. Madam, I fear
Your too deep sense of grief has turned your reason.

CLEOPATRA. No, no, I'm not run mad; I can bear fortune:
And love may be expelled by other love,
As poisons are by poisons.

DOLABELLA. You o'erjoy me, madam,
To find your griefs so moderately borne.
You've heard the worst; all are not false like him.

CLEOPATRA. No; Heaven forbid they should.

DOLABELLA. Some men are constant.

CLEOPATRA. And constancy deserves reward, that's certain.

DOLABELLA. Deserves it not; but give it leave to hope.

VENTIDIUS. I'll swear, thou hast my leave. I have enough:
But how to manage this! Well, I'll consider.
    [Exit.]

DOLABELLA. I came prepared
To tell you heavy news; news, which I thought
Would fright the blood from your pale cheeks to hear:
But you have met it with a cheerfulness,
That makes my task more easy; and my tongue,
Which on another's message was employed,
Would gladly speak its own.

CLEOPATRA. Hold, Dolabella.
First tell me, were you chosen by my lord?
Or sought you this employment?

DOLABELLA. He picked me out; and, as his bosom friend,
He charged me with his words.

CLEOPATRA. The message then
I know was tender, and each accent smooth,

To mollify that rugged word, DEPART.

DOLABELLA. Oh, you mistake: He chose the harshest words;
With fiery eyes, and contracted brows,
He coined his face in the severest stamp;
And fury shook his fabric, like an earthquake;
He heaved for vent, and burst like bellowing Aetna,
In sounds scarce human — "Hence away for ever,
Let her begone, the blot of my renown,
And bane of all my hopes!"
    [All the time of this speech, CLEOPATRA seems more
    and more concerned, till she sinks quite down.]
"Let her be driven, as far as men can think,
From man's commerce! she'll poison to the centre."

CLEOPATRA. Oh, I can bear no more!

DOLABELLA. Help, help! — O wretch! O cursed, cursed wretch!
What have I done!

CHARMION. Help, chafe her temples, Iras.

IRAS. Bend, bend her forward quickly.

CHARMION. Heaven be praised,
She comes again.

CLEOPATRA. Oh, let him not approach me.
Why have you brought me back to this loathed being;
The abode of falsehood, violated vows,
And injured love? For pity, let me go;
For, if there be a place of long repose,
I'm sure I want it. My disdainful lord
Can never break that quiet; nor awake
The sleeping soul, with hollowing in my tomb
Such words as fright her hence. — Unkind, unkind!

DOLABELLA. Believe me, 'tis against myself I speak;
   [Kneeling.]
That sure desires belief; I injured him:
My friend ne'er spoke those words. Oh, had you seen
How often he came back, and every time
With something more obliging and more kind,
To add to what he said; what dear farewells;
How almost vanquished by his love he parted,
And leaned to what unwillingly he left!
I, traitor as I was, for love of you
(But what can you not do, who made me false?)
I forged that lie; for whose forgiveness kneels
This self-accused, self-punished criminal.

CLEOPATRA. With how much ease believe we what we wish!
Rise, Dolabella; if you have been guilty,
I have contributed, and too much love
Has made me guilty too.
The advance of kindness, which I made, was feigned,
To call back fleeting love by jealousy;
But 'twould not last. Oh, rather let me lose,
Than so ignobly trifle with his heart.

DOLABELLA. I find your breast fenced round from human reach,
Transparent as a rock of solid crystal;
Seen through, but never pierced. My friend, my friend,
What endless treasure hast thou thrown away;
And scattered, like an infant, in the ocean,
Vain sums of wealth, which none can gather thence!

CLEOPATRA. Could you not beg
An hour's admittance to his private ear?
Like one, who wanders through long barren wilds
And yet foreknows no hospitable inn
Is near to succour hunger, eats his fill,
Before his painful march;
So would I feed a while my famished eyes

Before we part; for I have far to go,
If death be far, and never must return.

VENTIDIUS with OCTAVIA, behind

VENTIDIUS. From hence you may discover—oh, sweet, sweet!
Would you indeed? The pretty hand in earnest?

DOLABELLA. I will, for this reward.
    [Takes her hand.]
Draw it not back.
'Tis all I e'er will beg.

  VENTIDIUS. They turn upon us.

  OCTAVIA. What quick eyes has guilt!

VENTIDIUS. Seem not to have observed them, and go on.
    [They enter.]

  DOLABELLA. Saw you the emperor, Ventidius?

VENTIDIUS. No.
I sought him; but I heard that he was private,
None with him but Hipparchus, his freedman.

  DOLABELLA. Know you his business?

VENTIDIUS. Giving him instructions,
And letters to his brother Caesar.

DOLABELLA. Well,
He must be found.
    [Exeunt DOLABELLA and CLEOPATRA.]

  OCTAVIA. Most glorious impudence!

VENTIDIUS. She looked, methought,
As she would say—Take your old man, Octavia;

Thank you, I'm better here.—
Well, but what use
Make we of this discovery?

  OCTAVIA. Let it die.

VENTIDIUS. I pity Dolabella; but she's dangerous:
Her eyes have power beyond Thessalian charms,
To draw the moon from heaven; for eloquence,
The sea-green Syrens taught her voice their flattery;
And, while she speaks, night steals upon the day,
Unmarked of those that hear. Then she's so charming,
Age buds at sight of her, and swells to youth:
The holy priests gaze on her when she smiles;
And with heaved hands, forgetting gravity,
They bless her wanton eyes: Even I, who hate her,
With a malignant joy behold such beauty;
And, while I curse, desire it. Antony
Must needs have some remains of passion still,
Which may ferment into a worse relapse,
If now not fully cured. I know, this minute,
With Caesar he's endeavouring her peace.

OCTAVIA. You have prevailed:—But for a further purpose
    [Walks off.]
I'll prove how he will relish this discovery.
What, make a strumpet's peace! it swells my heart:
It must not, shall not be.

VENTIDIUS. His guards appear.
Let me begin, and you shall second me.

  Enter ANTONY

ANTONY. Octavia, I was looking you, my love:
What, are your letters ready? I have given
My last instructions.

OCTAVIA. Mine, my lord, are written.

ANTONY. Ventidius.
 [Drawing him aside.]

 VENTIDIUS. My lord?

ANTONY. A word in private.—
When saw you Dolabella?

VENTIDIUS. Now, my lord,
He parted hence; and Cleopatra with him.

ANTONY. Speak softly.—'Twas by my command he went,
To bear my last farewell.

VENTIDIUS. It looked indeed
 [Aloud.]
Like your farewell.

ANTONY. More softly.—My farewell?
What secret meaning have you in those words
Of—My farewell? He did it by my order.

VENTIDIUS. Then he obeyed your order. I suppose
 [Aloud.]
You bid him do it with all gentleness,
All kindness, and all—love.

ANTONY. How she mourned,
The poor forsaken creature!

VENTIDIUS. She took it as she ought; she bore your parting
As she did Caesar's, as she would another's,
Were a new love to come.

ANTONY. Thou dost belie her;
    [Aloud.]
Most basely, and maliciously belie her.

 VENTIDIUS. I thought not to displease you; I have done.

OCTAVIA. You seemed disturbed, my Lord.
    [Coming up.]

ANTONY. A very trifle.
Retire, my love.

VENTIDIUS. It was indeed a trifle.
He sent —

ANTONY. No more. Look how thou disobey'st me;
    [Angrily.]
Thy life shall answer it.

 OCTAVIA. Then 'tis no trifle.

VENTIDIUS. [to OCTAVIA.]
'Tis less; a very nothing: You too saw it,
As well as I, and therefore 'tis no secret.

 ANTONY. She saw it!

 VENTIDIUS. Yes: She saw young Dolabella —

 ANTONY. Young Dolabella!

VENTIDIUS. Young, I think him young,
And handsome too; and so do others think him.
But what of that? He went by your command,
Indeed 'tis probable, with some kind message;
For she received it graciously; she smiled;
And then he grew familiar with her hand,
Squeezed it, and worried it with ravenous kisses;
She blushed, and sighed, and smiled, and blushed again;

At last she took occasion to talk softly,
And brought her cheek up close, and leaned on his;
At which, he whispered kisses back on hers;
And then she cried aloud — That constancy
Should be rewarded.

OCTAVIA. This I saw and heard.

ANTONY. What woman was it, whom you heard and saw
So playful with my friend?
Not Cleopatra?

VENTIDIUS. Even she, my lord.

ANTONY. My Cleopatra?

VENTIDIUS. Your Cleopatra;
Dolabella's Cleopatra; every man's Cleopatra.

ANTONY. Thou liest.

VENTIDIUS. I do not lie, my lord.
Is this so strange? Should mistresses be left,
And not provide against a time of change?
You know she's not much used to lonely nights.

ANTONY. I'll think no more on't.
I know 'tis false, and see the plot betwixt you. —
You needed not have gone this way, Octavia.
What harms it you that Cleopatra's just?
She's mine no more. I see, and I forgive:
Urge it no further, love.

OCTAVIA. Are you concerned,
That she's found false?

ANTONY. I should be, were it so;
For, though 'tis past, I would not that the world

Should tax my former choice, that I loved one
Of so light note; but I forgive you both.

VENTIDIUS. What has my age deserved, that you should think
I would abuse your ears with perjury?
If Heaven be true, she's false.

ANTONY. Though heaven and earth
Should witness it, I'll not believe her tainted.

VENTIDIUS. I'll bring you, then, a witness
From hell, to prove her so. — Nay, go not back;
  [Seeing ALEXAS just entering, and starting back.]
For stay you must and shall.

  ALEXAS. What means my lord?

VENTIDIUS. To make you do what most you hate, — speak truth.
You are of Cleopatra's private counsel,
Of her bed-counsel, her lascivious hours;
Are conscious of each nightly change she makes,
And watch her, as Chaldaeans do the moon,
Can tell what signs she passes through, what day.

  ALEXAS. My noble lord!

VENTIDIUS. My most illustrious pander,
No fine set speech, no cadence, no turned periods,
But a plain homespun truth, is what I ask.
I did, myself, o'erhear your queen make love
To Dolabella. Speak; for I will know,
By your confession, what more passed betwixt them;
How near the business draws to your employment;
And when the happy hour.

ANTONY. Speak truth, Alexas; whether it offend
Or please Ventidius, care not: Justify

Thy injured queen from malice: Dare his worst.

OCTAVIA. [aside.] See how he gives him courage! how he fears
To find her false! and shuts his eyes to truth,
Willing to be misled!

ALEXAS. As far as love may plead for woman's frailty,
Urged by desert and greatness of the lover,
So far, divine Octavia, may my queen
Stand even excused to you for loving him
Who is your lord: so far, from brave Ventidius,
May her past actions hope a fair report.

ANTONY. 'Tis well, and truly spoken: mark, Ventidius.

ALEXAS. To you, most noble emperor, her strong passion
Stands not excused, but wholly justified.
Her beauty's charms alone, without her crown,
From Ind and Meroe drew the distant vows
Of sighing kings; and at her feet were laid
The sceptres of the earth, exposed on heaps,
To choose where she would reign:
She thought a Roman only could deserve her,
And, of all Romans, only Antony;
And, to be less than wife to you, disdained
Their lawful passion.

ANTONY. 'Tis but truth.

ALEXAS. And yet, though love, and your unmatched desert,
Have drawn her from the due regard of honour,
At last Heaven opened her unwilling eyes
To see the wrongs she offered fair Octavia,
Whose holy bed she lawlessly usurped.
The sad effects of this improsperous war
Confirmed those pious thoughts.

VENTIDIUS. [aside.] Oh, wheel you there?
Observe him now; the man begins to mend,
And talk substantial reason. — Fear not, eunuch;
The emperor has given thee leave to speak.

ALEXAS. Else had I never dared to offend his ears
With what the last necessity has urged
On my forsaken mistress; yet I must not
Presume to say, her heart is wholly altered.

ANTONY. No, dare not for thy life, I charge thee dare not
Pronounce that fatal word!

OCTAVIA. Must I bear this? Good Heaven, afford me patience.
    [Aside.]

 VENTIDIUS. On, sweet eunuch; my dear half-man, proceed.

ALEXAS. Yet Dolabella
Has loved her long; he, next my god-like lord,
Deserves her best; and should she meet his passion,
Rejected, as she is, by him she loved — —

ANTONY. Hence from my sight! for I can bear no more:
Let furies drag thee quick to hell; let all
The longer damned have rest; each torturing hand
Do thou employ, till Cleopatra comes;
Then join thou too, and help to torture her!
    [Exit ALEXAS, thrust out by ANTONY.]

OCTAVIA. 'Tis not well.
Indeed, my lord, 'tis much unkind to me,
To show this passion, this extreme concernment,
For an abandoned, faithless prostitute.

ANTONY. Octavia, leave me; I am much disordered:
Leave me, I say.

OCTAVIA. My lord!

ANTONY. I bid you leave me.

VENTIDIUS. Obey him, madam: best withdraw a while,
And see how this will work.

OCTAVIA. Wherein have I offended you, my lord,
That I am bid to leave you? Am I false,
Or infamous? Am I a Cleopatra?
Were I she,
Base as she is, you would not bid me leave you;
But hang upon my neck, take slight excuses,
And fawn upon my falsehood.

ANTONY. 'Tis too much.
Too much, Octavia; I am pressed with sorrows
Too heavy to be borne; and you add more:
I would retire, and recollect what's left
Of man within, to aid me.

OCTAVIA. You would mourn,
In private, for your love, who has betrayed you.
You did but half return to me: your kindness
Lingered behind with her, I hear, my lord,
You make conditions for her,
And would include her treaty. Wondrous proofs
Of love to me!

ANTONY. Are you my friend, Ventidius?
Or are you turned a Dolabella too,
And let this fury loose?

VENTIDIUS. Oh, be advised,
Sweet madam, and retire.

OCTAVIA. Yes, I will go; but never to return.
You shall no more be haunted with this Fury.
My lord, my lord, love will not always last,
When urged with long unkindness and disdain:
Take her again, whom you prefer to me;
She stays but to be called. Poor cozened man!
Let a feigned parting give her back your heart,
Which a feigned love first got; for injured me,
Though my just sense of wrongs forbid my stay,
My duty shall be yours.
To the dear pledges of our former love
My tenderness and care shall be transferred,
And they shall cheer, by turns, my widowed nights:
So, take my last farewell; for I despair
To have you whole, and scorn to take you half.
    [Exit.]

VENTIDIUS. I combat Heaven, which blasts my best designs;
My last attempt must be to win her back;
But oh! I fear in vain.
    [Exit.]

ANTONY. Why was I framed with this plain, honest heart,
Which knows not to disguise its griefs and weakness,
But bears its workings outward to the world?
I should have kept the mighty anguish in,
And forced a smile at Cleopatra's falsehood:
Octavia had believed it, and had stayed.
But I am made a shallow-forded stream,
Seen to the bottom: all my clearness scorned,
And all my faults exposed. —See where he comes,

Enter DOLLABELLA

Who has profaned the sacred name of friend,
And worn it into vileness!
With how secure a brow, and specious form,
He gilds the secret villain! Sure that face
Was meant for honesty; but Heaven mismatched it,
And furnished treason out with nature's pomp,
To make its work more easy.

DOLABELLA. O my friend!

ANTONY. Well, Dolabella, you performed my message?

DOLABELLA. I did, unwillingly.

ANTONY. Unwillingly?
Was it so hard for you to bear our parting?
You should have wished it.

DOLABELLA. Why?

ANTONY. Because you love me.
And she received my message with as true,
With as unfeigned a sorrow as you brought it?

DOLABELLA. She loves you, even to madness.

ANTONY. Oh, I know it.
You, Dolabella, do not better know
How much she loves me. And should I
Forsake this beauty? This all-perfect creature?

DOLABELLA. I could not, were she mine.

ANTONY. And yet you first
Persuaded me: How come you altered since?

DOLABELLA. I said at first I was not fit to go:
I could not hear her sighs, and see her tears,
But pity must prevail: And so, perhaps,
It may again with you; for I have promised,

That she should take her last farewell: And, see,
She comes to claim my word.

Enter CLEOPATRA

ANTONY. False Dolabella!

DOLABELLA. What's false, my lord?

ANTONY. Why, Dolabella's false,
And Cleopatra's false; both false and faithless.
Draw near, you well-joined wickedness, you serpents,
Whom I have in my kindly bosom warmed,
Till I am stung to death.

DOLABELLA. My lord, have I
Deserved to be thus used?

CLEOPATRA. Can Heaven prepare
A newer torment? Can it find a curse
Beyond our separation?

ANTONY. Yes, if fate
Be just, much greater: Heaven should be ingenious
In punishing such crimes. The rolling stone,
And gnawing vulture, were slight pains, invented
When Jove was young, and no examples known
Of mighty ills; but you have ripened sin,
To such a monstrous growth, 'twill pose the gods
To find an equal torture. Two, two such!—
Oh, there's no further name,—two such! to me,
To me, who locked my soul within your breasts,
Had no desires, no joys, no life, but you;
When half the globe was mine, I gave it you
In dowry with my heart; I had no use,
No fruit of all, but you: A friend and mistress
Was what the world could give. O Cleopatra!
O Dolabella! how could you betray

This tender heart, which with an infant fondness
Lay lulled betwixt your bosoms, and there slept,
Secure of injured faith?

DOLABELLA. If she has wronged you,
Heaven, hell, and you revenge it.

ANTONY. If she has wronged me!
Thou wouldst evade thy part of guilt; but swear
Thou lov'st not her.

DOLABELLA. Not so as I love you.

ANTONY. Not so? Swear, swear, I say, thou dost not love her.

DOLABELLA. No more than friendship will allow.

ANTONY. No more?
Friendship allows thee nothing: Thou art perjured—
And yet thou didst not swear thou lov'st her not;
But not so much, no more. O trifling hypocrite,
Who dar'st not own to her, thou dost not love,
Nor own to me, thou dost! Ventidius heard it;
Octavia saw it.

CLEOPATRA. They are enemies.

ANTONY. Alexas is not so: He, he confessed it;
He, who, next hell, best knew it, he avowed it.
Why do I seek a proof beyond yourself?
   [To DOLABELLA.]
You, whom I sent to bear my last farewell,
Returned, to plead her stay.

DOLABELLA. What shall I answer?
If to have loved be guilt, then I have sinned;
But if to have repented of that love
Can wash away my crime, I have repented.
Yet, if I have offended past forgiveness,

Let not her suffer: She is innocent.

CLEOPATRA. Ah, what will not a woman do, who loves?
What means will she refuse, to keep that heart,
Where all her joys are placed? 'Twas I encouraged,
'Twas I blew up the fire that scorched his soul,
To make you jealous, and by that regain you.
But all in vain; I could not counterfeit:
In spite of all the dams my love broke o'er,
And drowned by heart again: fate took the occasion;
And thus one minute's feigning has destroyed
My whole life's truth.

ANTONY. Thin cobweb arts of falsehood;
Seen, and broke through at first.

DOLABELLA. Forgive your mistress.

CLEOPATRA. Forgive your friend.

ANTONY. You have convinced yourselves.
You plead each other's cause: What witness have you,
That you but meant to raise my jealousy?

CLEOPATRA. Ourselves, and Heaven.

ANTONY. Guilt witnesses for guilt. Hence, love and friendship!
You have no longer place in human breasts,
These two have driven you out: Avoid my sight!
I would not kill the man whom I have loved,
And cannot hurt the woman; but avoid me:
I do not know how long I can be tame;
For, if I stay one minute more, to think
How I am wronged, my justice and revenge
Will cry so loud within me, that my pity
Will not be heard for either.

DOLABELLA. Heaven has but
Our sorrow for our sins; and then delights
To pardon erring man: Sweet mercy seems
Its darling attribute, which limits justice;
As if there were degrees in infinite,
And infinite would rather want perfection
Than punish to extent.

ANTONY. I can forgive
A foe; but not a mistress and a friend.
Treason is there in its most horrid shape,
Where trust is greatest; and the soul resigned,
Is stabbed by its own guards: I'll hear no more;
Hence from my sight for ever!

CLEOPATRA. How? for ever!
I cannot go one moment from your sight,
And must I go for ever?
My joys, my only joys, are centred here:
What place have I to go to? My own kingdom?
That I have lost for you: Or to the Romans?
They hate me for your sake: Or must I wander
The wide world o'er, a helpless, banished woman,
Banished for love of you; banished from you?
Ay, there's the banishment! Oh, hear me; hear me,
With strictest justice: For I beg no favour;
And if I have offended you, then kill me,
But do not banish me.

ANTONY. I must not hear you.
I have a fool within me takes your part;
But honour stops my ears.

CLEOPATRA. For pity hear me!
Would you cast off a slave who followed you?
Who crouched beneath your spurn? — He has no pity!
See, if he gives one tear to my departure;

One look, one kind farewell: O iron heart!
Let all the gods look down, and judge betwixt us,
If he did ever love!

  ANTONY. No more: Alexas!

  DOLABELLA. A perjured villain!

  ANTONY. [to CLEOPATRA.] Your Alexas; yours.

CLEOPATRA. Oh, 'twas his plot; his ruinous design,
To engage you in my love by jealousy.
Hear him; confront him with me; let him speak.

  ANTONY. I have; I have.

  CLEOPATRA. And if he clear me not —

ANTONY. Your creature! one, who hangs upon your smiles!
Watches your eye, to say or to unsay,
Whate'er you please! I am not to be moved.

CLEOPATRA. Then must we part? Farewell, my cruel lord!
The appearance is against me; and I go,
Unjustified, for ever from your sight.
How I have loved, you know; how yet I love,
My only comfort is, I know myself:
I love you more, even now you are unkind,
Then when you loved me most; so well, so truly
I'll never strive against it; but die pleased,
To think you once were mine.

ANTONY. Good heaven, they weep at parting!
Must I weep too? that calls them innocent.
I must not weep; and yet I must, to think
That I must not forgive. —
Live, but live wretched; 'tis but just you should,
Who made me so: Live from each other's sight:
Let me not hear you meet. Set all the earth,
And all the seas, betwixt your sundered loves:

View nothing common but the sun and skies.
Now, all take several ways;
  And each your own sad fate, with mine, deplore;
  That you were false, and I could trust no more.
    [Exeunt severally.]

Act V

Scene I

Enter CLEOPATRA, CHARMION, and IRAS

CHARMION. Be juster, Heaven; such virtue punished thus,
Will make us think that chance rules all above,
And shuffles, with a random hand, the lots,
Which man is forced to draw.

CLEOPATRA. I could tear out these eyes, that gained his heart,
And had not power to keep it. O the curse
Of doting on, even when I find it dotage!
Bear witness, gods, you heard him bid me go;
You, whom he mocked with imprecating vows
Of promised faith! — I'll die; I will not bear it.
You may hold me —
    [She pulls out her dagger, and they hold her.]
But I can keep my breath; I can die inward,
And choke this love.

Enter ALEXAS

IRAS. Help, O Alexas, help!
The queen grows desperate; her soul struggles in her
With all the agonies of love and rage,
And strives to force its passage.

CLEOPATRA. Let me go.
Art thou there, traitor!—O,
O for a little breath, to vent my rage,
Give, give me way, and let me loose upon him.

ALEXAS. Yes, I deserve it, for my ill-timed truth.
Was it for me to prop
The ruins of a falling majesty?
To place myself beneath the mighty flaw,
Thus to be crushed, and pounded into atoms,
By its o'erwhelming weight? 'Tis too presuming
For subjects to preserve that wilful power,
Which courts its own destruction.

CLEOPATRA. I would reason
More calmly with you. Did not you o'errule,
And force my plain, direct, and open love,
Into these crooked paths of jealousy?
Now, what's the event? Octavia is removed;
But Cleopatra's banished. Thou, thou villain,
Hast pushed my boat to open sea; to prove,
At my sad cost, if thou canst steer it back.
It cannot be; I'm lost too far; I'm ruined:
Hence, thou impostor, traitor, monster, devil!—
I can no more: Thou, and my griefs, have sunk
Me down so low, that I want voice to curse thee.

ALEXAS. Suppose some shipwrecked seaman near the shore,
Dropping and faint, with climbing up the cliff,
If, from above, some charitable hand
Pull him to safety, hazarding himself,
To draw the other's weight; would he look back,
And curse him for his pains? The case is yours;
But one step more, and you have gained the height.

  CLEOPATRA. Sunk, never more to rise.

ALEXAS. Octavia's gone, and Dolabella banished.
Believe me, madam, Antony is yours.
His heart was never lost, but started off
To jealousy, love's last retreat and covert;
Where it lies hid in shades, watchful in silence,
And listening for the sound that calls it back.
Some other, any man ('tis so advanced),
May perfect this unfinished work, which I
(Unhappy only to myself) have left
So easy to his hand.

CLEOPATRA. Look well thou do't; else—

ALEXAS. Else, what your silence threatens.—Antony
Is mounted up the Pharos; from whose turret,
He stands surveying our Egyptian galleys,
Engaged with Caesar's fleet. Now death or conquest!
If the first happen, fate acquits my promise;
If we o'ercome, the conqueror is yours.
    [A distant shout within.]

CHARMION. Have comfort, madam: Did you mark that shout?
    [Second shout nearer.]

IRAS. Hark! they redouble it.

ALEXAS. 'Tis from the port.
The loudness shows it near: Good news, kind heavens!

CLEOPATRA. Osiris make it so!

Enter SERAPION

SERAPION. Where, where's the queen?

ALEXAS. How frightfully the holy coward stares
As if not yet recovered of the assault,
When all his gods, and, what's more dear to him,
His offerings, were at stake.

SERAPION. O horror, horror!
Egypt has been; our latest hour has come:
The queen of nations, from her ancient seat,
Is sunk for ever in the dark abyss:
Time has unrolled her glories to the last,
And now closed up the volume.

CLEOPATRA. Be more plain:
Say, whence thou comest; though fate is in thy face,
Which from the haggard eyes looks wildly out,
And threatens ere thou speakest.

SERAPION. I came from Pharos;
From viewing (spare me, and imagine it)
Our land's last hope, your navy —

 CLEOPATRA. Vanquished?

SERAPION. No:
They fought not.

 CLEOPATRA. Then they fled.

SERAPION. Nor that. I saw,
With Antony, your well-appointed fleet
Row out; and thrice he waved his hand on high,
And thrice with cheerful cries they shouted back:
'Twas then false Fortune, like a fawning strumpet,
About to leave the bankrupt prodigal,
With a dissembled smile would kiss at parting,
And flatter to the last; the well-timed oars,
Now dipt from every bank, now smoothly run
To meet the foe; and soon indeed they met,
But not as foes. In few, we saw their caps
On either side thrown up; the Egyptian galleys,
Received like friends, passed through, and fell behind
The Roman rear: And now, they all come forward,

And ride within the port.

CLEOPATRA. Enough, Serapion:
I've heard my doom. — This needed not, you gods:
When I lost Antony, your work was done;
'Tis but superfluous malice. — Where's my lord?
How bears he this last blow?

SERAPION. His fury cannot be expressed by words:
Thrice he attempted headlong to have fallen
Full on his foes, and aimed at Caesar's galley:
Withheld, he raves on you; cries, — He's betrayed.
Should he now find you —

ALEXAS. Shun him; seek your safety,
Till you can clear your innocence.

CLEOPATRA. I'll stay.

ALEXAS. You must not; haste you to your monument,
While I make speed to Caesar.

CLEOPATRA. Caesar! No,
I have no business with him.

ALEXAS. I can work him
To spare your life, and let this madman perish.

CLEOPATRA. Base fawning wretch! wouldst thou betray him too?
Hence from my sight! I will not hear a traitor;
'Twas thy design brought all this ruin on us. —
Serapion, thou art honest; counsel me:
But haste, each moment's precious.

SERAPION. Retire; you must not yet see Antony.
He who began this mischief,
'Tis just he tempt the danger; let him clear you:
And, since he offered you his servile tongue,
To gain a poor precarious life from Caesar,
Let him expose that fawning eloquence,
And speak to Antony.

ALEXAS. O heavens! I dare not;
I meet my certain death.

CLEOPATRA. Slave, thou deservest it. —
Not that I fear my lord, will I avoid him;
I know him noble: when he banished me,
And thought me false, he scorned to take my life;
But I'll be justified, and then die with him.

 ALEXAS. O pity me, and let me follow you.

CLEOPATRA. To death, if thou stir hence. Speak, if thou canst,
Now for thy life, which basely thou wouldst save;
While mine I prize at—this! Come, good Serapion.
    [Exeunt CLEOPATRA, SERAPION, CHARMION, and IRAS.]

ALEXAS. O that I less could fear to lose this being,
Which, like a snowball in my coward hand,
The more 'tis grasped, the faster melts away.
Poor reason! what a wretched aid art thou!
For still, in spite of thee,
These two long lovers, soul and body, dread
Their final separation. Let me think:
What can I say, to save myself from death?
No matter what becomes of Cleopatra.

ANTONY. Which way? where?
    [Within.]

VENTIDIUS. This leads to the monument.
   [Within.]

ALEXAS. Ah me! I hear him; yet I'm unprepared:
My gift of lying's gone;
And this court-devil, which I so oft have raised,
Forsakes me at my need. I dare not stay;
Yet cannot far go hence.
   [Exit.]

  Enter ANTONY and VENTIDIUS

ANTONY. O happy Caesar! thou hast men to lead:
Think not 'tis thou hast conquered Antony;
But Rome has conquered Egypt. I'm betrayed.

VENTIDIUS. Curse on this treacherous train!
Their soil and heaven infect them all with baseness:
And their young souls come tainted to the world
With the first breath they draw.

ANTONY. The original villain sure no god created;
He was a bastard of the sun, by Nile,
Aped into man; with all his mother's mud
Crusted about his soul.

VENTIDIUS. The nation is
One universal traitor; and their queen
The very spirit and extract of them all.

ANTONY. Is there yet left
A possibility of aid from valour?
Is there one god unsworn to my destruction?
The least unmortgaged hope? for, if there be,
Methinks I cannot fall beneath the fate
Of such a boy as Caesar.

The world's one half is yet in Antony;
And from each limb of it, that's hewed away,
The soul comes back to me.

VENTIDIUS. There yet remain
Three legions in the town. The last assault
Lopt off the rest; if death be your design, —
As I must wish it now, — these are sufficient
To make a heap about us of dead foes,
An honest pile for burial.

ANTONY. They are enough.
We'll not divide our stars; but, side by side,
Fight emulous, and with malicious eyes
Survey each other's acts: So every death
Thou giv'st, I'll take on me, as a just debt,
And pay thee back a soul.

VENTIDIUS. Now you shall see I love you. Not a word
Of chiding more. By my few hours of life,
I am so pleased with this brave Roman fate,
That I would not be Caesar, to outlive you.
When we put off this flesh, and mount together,
I shall be shown to all the ethereal crowd, —
Lo, this is he who died with Antony!

ANTONY. Who knows, but we may pierce through all their tro-
ops,
And reach my veterans yet? 'tis worth the 'tempting,
To o'erleap this gulf of fate,
And leave our wandering destinies behind.

Enter ALEXAS, trembling

VENTIDIUS. See, see, that villain!
See Cleopatra stamped upon that face,
With all her cunning, all her arts of falsehood!

How she looks out through those dissembling eyes!
How he sets his countenance for deceit,
And promises a lie, before he speaks!
Let me despatch him first.
    [Drawing.]

  ALEXAS. O spare me, spare me!

ANTONY. Hold; he's not worth your killing.—On thy life,
Which thou may'st keep, because I scorn to take it,
No syllable to justify thy queen;
Save thy base tongue its office.

ALEXAS. Sir, she is gone.
Where she shall never be molested more
By love, or you.

ANTONY. Fled to her Dolabella!
Die, traitor! I revoke my promise! die!
    [Going to kill him.]

  ALEXAS. O hold! she is not fled.

ANTONY. She is: my eyes
Are open to her falsehood; my whole life
Has been a golden dream of love and friendship;
But, now I wake, I'm like a merchant, roused
From soft repose, to see his vessel sinking,
And all his wealth cast over. Ungrateful woman!
Who followed me, but as the swallow summer,
Hatching her young ones in my kindly beams,
Singing her flatteries to my morning wake:
But, now my winter comes, she spreads her wings,
And seeks the spring of Caesar.

ALEXAS. Think not so;
Her fortunes have, in all things, mixed with yours.

Had she betrayed her naval force to Rome,
How easily might she have gone to Caesar,
Secure by such a bribe!

VENTIDIUS. She sent it first,
To be more welcome after.

ANTONY. 'Tis too plain;
Else would she have appeared, to clear herself.

ALEXAS. Too fatally she has: she could not bear
To be accused by you; but shut herself
Within her monument; looked down and sighed;
While, from her unchanged face, the silent tears
Dropt, as they had not leave, but stole their parting.
Some indistinguished words she only murmured;
At last, she raised her eyes; and, with such looks
As dying Lucrece cast—

ANTONY. My heart forebodes—

VENTIDIUS. All for the best:—Go on.

ALEXAS. She snatched her poniard,
And, ere we could prevent the fatal blow,
Plunged it within her breast; then turned to me:
Go, bear my lord, said she, my last farewell;
And ask him, if he yet suspect my faith.
More she was saying, but death rushed betwixt.
She half pronounced your name with her last breath,
And buried half within her.

VENTIDIUS. Heaven be praised!

ANTONY. Then art thou innocent, my poor dear love,
And art thou dead?
O those two words! their sound should be divided:
Hadst thou been false, and died; or hadst thou lived,

And hadst been true—But innocence and death!
This shows not well above. Then what am I,
The murderer of this truth, this innocence!
Thoughts cannot form themselves in words so horrid
As can express my guilt!

VENTIDIUS. Is't come to this? The gods have been too gracious;
And thus you thank them for it!

ANTONY. [to ALEXAS.] Why stayest thou here?
Is it for thee to spy upon my soul,
And see its inward mourning? Get thee hence;
Thou art not worthy to behold, what now
Becomes a Roman emperor to perform.

ALEXAS. He loves her still:
His grief betrays it. Good! the joy to find
She's yet alive, completes the reconcilement.
I've saved myself, and her. But, oh! the Romans!
Fate comes too fast upon my wit,
Hunts me too hard, and meets me at each double.
    [Aside.]
    [Exit.]

VENTIDIUS. Would she had died a little sooner, though!
Before Octavia went, you might have treated:
Now 'twill look tame, and would not be received.
Come, rouse yourself, and let's die warm together.

ANTONY. I will not fight: there's no more work for war.
The business of my angry hours is done.

   VENTIDIUS. Caesar is at your gates.

ANTONY. Why, let him enter;
He's welcome now.

VENTIDIUS. What lethargy has crept into your soul?

ANTONY. 'Tis but a scorn of life, and just desire
To free myself from bondage.

VENTIDIUS. Do it bravely.

ANTONY. I will; but not by fighting. O Ventidius!
What should I fight for now? — my queen is dead.
I was but great for her; my power, my empire,
Were but my merchandise to buy her love;
And conquered kings, my factors. Now she's dead,
Let Caesar take the world, —
An empty circle, since the jewel's gone
Which made it worth my strife: my being's nauseous;
For all the bribes of life are gone away.

VENTIDIUS. Would you be taken?

ANTONY. Yes, I would be taken;
But, as a Roman ought, — dead, my Ventidius:
For I'll convey my soul from Caesar's reach,
And lay down life myself. 'Tis time the world
Should have a lord, and know whom to obey.
We two have kept its homage in suspense,
And bent the globe, on whose each side we trod,
Till it was dented inwards. Let him walk
Alone upon't: I'm weary of my part.
My torch is out; and the world stands before me,
Like a black desert at the approach of night:
I'll lay me down, and stray no farther on.

VENTIDIUS. I could be grieved,
But that I'll not outlive you: choose your death;
For, I have seen him in such various shapes,

I care not which I take: I'm only troubled,
The life I bear is worn to such a rag,
'Tis scarce worth giving. I could wish, indeed,
We threw it from us with a better grace;
That, like two lions taken in the toils,
We might at last thrust out our paws, and wound
The hunters that inclose us.

ANTONY. I have thought on it.
Ventidius, you must live.

VENTIDIUS. I must not, sir.

ANTONY. Wilt thou not live, to speak some good of me?
To stand by my fair fame, and guard the approaches
From the ill tongues of men?

VENTIDIUS. Who shall guard mine,
For living after you?

ANTONY. Say, I command it.

VENTIDIUS. If we die well, our deaths will speak themselves
And need no living witness.

ANTONY. Thou hast loved me,
And fain I would reward thee. I must die;
Kill me, and take the merit of my death,
To make thee friends with Caesar.

VENTIDIUS. Thank your kindness.
You said I loved you; and in recompense,
You bid me turn a traitor: Did I think
You would have used me thus? — that I should die
With a hard thought of you?

ANTONY. Forgive me, Roman.
Since I have heard of Cleopatra's death,
My reason bears no rule upon my tongue,
But lets my thoughts break all at random out.
I've thought better; do not deny me twice.

VENTIDIUS. By Heaven I will not.
Let it not be to outlive you.

ANTONY. Kill me first,
And then die thou; for 'tis but just thou serve
Thy friend, before thyself.

VENTIDIUS. Give me your hand.
We soon shall meet again. Now, farewell, emperor!—
    [Embrace.]
Methinks that word's too cold to be my last:
Since death sweeps all distinctions, farewell, friend!
That's all—
I will not make a business of a trifle;
And yet I cannot look on you, and kill you;
Pray turn your face.

  ANTONY. I do: strike home, be sure.

VENTIDIUS. Home as my sword will reach.
    [Kills himself.]

ANTONY. Oh, thou mistak'st;
That wound was not of thine; give it me back:
Thou robb'st me of my death.

VENTIDIUS. I do indeed;
But think 'tis the first time I e'er deceived you,
If that may plead my pardon.—And you, gods,
Forgive me, if you will; for I die perjured,

Rather than kill my friend.
    [Dies.]

ANTONY. Farewell! Ever my leader, even in death!
My queen and thou have got the start of me,
And I'm the lag of honour. — Gone so soon?
Is Death no more? he used him carelessly,
With a familiar kindness: ere he knocked,
Ran to the door, and took him in his arms,
As who should say — You're welcome at all hours,
A friend need give no warning. Books had spoiled him;
For all the learned are cowards by profession.
'Tis not worth
My further thought; for death, for aught I know,
Is but to think no more. Here's to be satisfied.
    [Falls on his sword.]
I've missed my heart. O unperforming hand!
Thou never couldst have erred in a worse time.
My fortune jades me to the last; and death,
Like a great man, takes state, and makes me wait
For my admittance. —
    [Trampling within.]
Some, perhaps, from Caesar:
If he should find me living, and suspect
That I played booty with my life! I'll mend
My work, ere they can reach me.
    [Rises upon his knees.]

Enter CLEOPATRA, CHARMION, and IRAS

CLEOPATRA. Where is my lord? where is he?

CHARMION. There he lies,
And dead Ventidius by him.

CLEOPATRA. My tears were prophets; I am come too late.
O that accursed Alexas!

[Runs to him.]

ANTONY. Art thou living?
Or am I dead before I knew, and thou
The first kind ghost that meets me?

CLEOPATRA. Help me seat him.
Send quickly, send for help!
    [They place him in a chair.]

ANTONY. I am answered.
We live both. Sit thee down, my Cleopatra:
I'll make the most I can of life, to stay
A moment more with thee.

 CLEOPATRA. How is it with you?

ANTONY. 'Tis as with a man
Removing in a hurry; all packed up,
But one dear jewel that his haste forgot;
And he, for that, returns upon the spur:
So I come back for thee.

CLEOPATRA. Too long, ye heavens, you have been cruel to me:
Now show your mended faith, and give me back
His fleeting life!

ANTONY. It will not be, my love;
I keep my soul by force.
Say but, thou art not false.

CLEOPATRA. 'Tis now too late
To say I'm true: I'll prove it, and die with you.
Unknown to me, Alexas feigned my death:
Which, when I knew, I hasted to prevent
This fatal consequence. My fleet betrayed

Both you and me.

ANTONY. And Dolabella—

CLEOPATRA. Scarce
Esteemed before he loved; but hated now.

ANTONY. Enough: my life's not long enough for more.
Thou say'st, thou wilt come after: I believe thee;
For I can now believe whate'er thou sayest,
That we may part more kindly.

CLEOPATRA. I will come:
Doubt not, my life, I'll come, and quickly too:
Caesar shall triumph o'er no part of thee.

ANTONY. But grieve not, while thou stayest,
My last disastrous times:
Think we have had a clear and glorious day
And Heaven did kindly to delay the storm,
Just till our close of evening. Ten years' love,
And not a moment lost, but all improved
To the utmost joys,—what ages have we lived?
And now to die each other's; and, so dying,
While hand in hand we walk in groves below,
Whole troops of lovers' ghosts shall flock about us,
And all the train be ours.

CLEOPATRA. Your words are like the notes of dying swans,
Too sweet to last. Were there so many hours
For your unkindness, and not one for love?

ANTONY. No, not a minute.—This one kiss—more worth
Than all I leave to Caesar.
    [Dies.]

CLEOPATRA. O tell me so again,
And take ten thousand kisses for that word.
My lord, my lord! speak, if you yet have being;
Sign to me, if you cannot speak; or cast
One look! Do anything that shows you live.

IRAS. He's gone too far to hear you;
And this you see, a lump of senseless clay,
The leavings of a soul.

CHARMION. Remember, madam,
He charged you not to grieve.

CLEOPATRA. And I'll obey him.
I have not loved a Roman, not to know
What should become his wife; his wife, my Charmion!
For 'tis to that high title I aspire;
And now I'll not die less. Let dull Octavia
Survive, to mourn him dead: My nobler fate
Shall knit our spousals with a tie, too strong
For Roman laws to break.

IRAS. Will you then die?

CLEOPATRA. Why shouldst thou make that question?

IRAS. Caesar is merciful.

CLEOPATRA. Let him be so
To those that want his mercy: My poor lord
Made no such covenant with him, to spare me
When he was dead. Yield me to Caesar's pride?
What! to be led in triumph through the streets,
A spectacle to base plebeian eyes;
While some dejected friend of Antony's,
Close in a corner, shakes his head, and mutters
A secret curse on her who ruined him!

I'll none of that.

CHARMION. Whatever you resolve,
I'll follow, even to death.

IRAS. I only feared
For you; but more should fear to live without you.

CLEOPATRA. Why, now, 'tis as it should be. Quick, my friends,
Despatch; ere this, the town's in Caesar's hands:
My lord looks down concerned, and fears my stay,
Lest I should be surprised;
Keep him not waiting for his love too long.
You, Charmion, bring my crown and richest jewels;
With them, the wreath of victory I made
(Vain augury!) for him, who now lies dead:
You, Iras, bring the cure of all our ills.

IRAS. The aspics, madam?

CLEOPATRA. Must I bid you twice?
    [Exit CHARMION and IRAS.]
'Tis sweet to die, when they would force life on me,
To rush into the dark abode of death,
And seize him first; if he be like my love,
He is not frightful, sure.
We're now alone, in secrecy and silence;
And is not this like lovers? I may kiss
These pale, cold lips; Octavia does not see me:
And, oh! 'tis better far to have him thus,
Than see him in her arms. — Oh, welcome, welcome!

Enter CHARMION and IRAS

CHARMION. What must be done?

CLEOPATRA. Short ceremony, friends;
But yet it must be decent. First, this laurel

Shall crown my hero's head: he fell not basely,
Nor left his shield behind him. — Only thou
Couldst triumph o'er thyself; and thou alone
Wert worthy so to triumph.

CHARMION. To what end
These ensigns of your pomp and royalty?

CLEOPATRA. Dull, that thou art! why 'tis to meet my love;
As when I saw him first, on Cydnus' bank,
All sparkling, like a goddess: so adorned,
I'll find him once again; my second spousals
Shall match my first in glory. Haste, haste, both,
And dress the bride of Antony.

 CHARMION. 'Tis done.

CLEOPATRA. Now seat me by my lord. I claim this place,
For I must conquer Caesar too, like him,
And win my share of the world. — Hail, you dear relics
Of my immortal love!
O let no impious hand remove you hence:
But rest for ever here! Let Egypt give
His death that peace, which it denied his life. —
Reach me the casket.

IRAS. Underneath the fruit
The aspic lies.

CLEOPATRA. Welcome, thou kind deceiver!
    [Putting aside the leaves.]
Thou best of thieves: who, with an easy key,
Dost open life, and, unperceived by us,
Even steal us from ourselves; discharging so
Death's dreadful office, better than himself;
Touching our limbs so gently into slumber,
That Death stands by, deceived by his own image,

And thinks himself but sleep.

SERAPION. The queen, where is she?
    [Within.]
The town is yielded, Caesar's at the gates.

CLEOPATRA. He comes too late to invade the rights of death!
Haste, bare my arm, and rouse the serpent's fury.
    [Holds out her arm, and draws it back.]
Coward flesh,
Wouldst thou conspire with Caesar to betray me,
As thou wert none of mine? I'll force thee to it,
And not be sent by him,
But bring, myself, my soul to Antony.
    [Turns aside, and then shows her arm bloody.]
Take hence; the work is done.

SERAPION. Break ope the door,
    [Within.]
And guard the traitor well.

  CHARMION. The next is ours.

IRAS. Now, Charmion, to be worthy
Of our great queen and mistress.
    [They apply the aspics.]

CLEOPATRA. Already, death, I feel thee in my veins:
I go with such a will to find my lord,
That we shall quickly meet.
A heavy numbness creeps through every limb,
And now 'tis at my head: My eyelids fall,
And my dear love is vanquished in a mist.
Where shall I find him, where? O turn me to him,
And lay me on his breast! — Caesar, thy worst;
Now part us, if thou canst.
    [Dies.]

[IRAS sinks down at her feet, and dies;
    CHARMION stands behind her chair, as dressing her head.]

Enter SERAPION, two PRIESTS, ALEXAS bound, EGYPTIANS

PRIEST. Behold, Serapion,
What havoc death has made!

SERAPION. 'Twas what I feared. —
Charmion, is this well done?

CHARMION. Yes, 'tis well done, and like a queen, the last
Of her great race: I follow her.
    [Sinks down: dies.]

ALEXAS. 'Tis true,
She has done well: Much better thus to die,
Than live to make a holiday in Rome.

SERAPION. See how the lovers sit in state together,
As they were giving laws to half mankind!
The impression of a smile, left in her face,
Shows she died pleased with him for whom she lived,
And went to charm him in another world.
Caesar's just entering: grief has now no leisure.
Secure that villain, as our pledge of safety,
To grace the imperial triumph. —Sleep, blest pair,
Secure from human chance, long ages out,
While all the storms of fate fly o'er your tomb;
  And fame to late posterity shall tell,
  No lovers lived so great, or died so well.
    [Exeunt.]

EPILOGUE

Poets, like disputants, when reasons fail,
Have one sure refuge left—and that's to rail.
Fop, coxcomb, fool, are thundered through the pit;
And this is all their equipage of wit.
We wonder how the devil this difference grows
Betwixt our fools in verse, and yours in prose:
For, 'faith, the quarrel rightly understood,
'Tis civil war with their own flesh and blood.
The threadbare author hates the gaudy coat;
And swears at the gilt coach, but swears afoot:
For 'tis observed of every scribbling man,
He grows a fop as fast as e'er he can;
Prunes up, and asks his oracle, the glass,
If pink or purple best become his face.
For our poor wretch, he neither rails nor prays;
Nor likes your wit just as you like his plays;
He has not yet so much of Mr. Bayes.
He does his best; and if he cannot please,
Would quietly sue out his WRIT OF EASE.
Yet, if he might his own grand jury call,
By the fair sex he begs to stand or fall.
Let Caesar's power the men's ambition move,
But grace you him who lost the world for love!
  Yet if some antiquated lady say,
The last age is not copied in his play;
Heaven help the man who for that face must drudge,
Which only has the wrinkles of a judge.
Let not the young and beauteous join with those;
For should you raise such numerous hosts of foes,
Young wits and sparks he to his aid must call;
'Tis more than one man's work to please you all.

0 1341 1463912 0

CPSIA information can be obtained at www.ICGtesting.com
Printed in the USA
LVOW101232210613

339670LV00001B/27/P

9 783842 441965